LAST DIAMOND ROSE

LAST DIAMOND ROSE

L.D. CARROLL

Leanna Carroll

CONTENTS

To those who have been made to feel lesser because of things out of their control. You have the power to live as you wish, and the stigma of others can never coerce you, as long as *you* know who you are.

PROLOGUE

* * *

You wanna know about her, then, huh? I knew she'd come up sooner or later.

Can't say I'm surprised you're interested in her. It's a bit of an understatement to say that living as a thirteen-year-old orphan with one arm really begs some interest, not to mention deflates her self-esteem. Not that anyone could tell, because this one was a firecracker, to say the least. Only I knew what was behind the surface because you're right, you know. I spent the most time with her out of anyone.

I met the young Diamond McMullen in the early days of her self-discovery when it seemed that things had turned up so far that they felt right back down again. Before that, she'd been in an orphanage of sorts, with a bunch of other young children that nobody wanted. These kids, well, you could say they were all *unique,* in the worst of ways. If you were looking for an unkempt youngin' with a poker flush selection of physical, psychological, or emotional issues, this place was what you called a "field day."

Diamond was a tough one, though. If you could say anything about her, that was it. Made it outta there, didn't she? And not just out of the home, neither. I'll tell you what I know, and you can do your psycho evaluation if you want to, but you won't find what you're looking for. I know, I'm gonna tell you anyway. I'm just lettin' you know you're wastin' your time.

Listen, if you're askin' for a story, pull up a chair, fellas. And I'll tell you what I know.

~ 1 ~

HOME SWEET HOME

Home? Yeah, that's a bit of a stretch.

I remember askin' Mrs. McMullen what she thought of the place where they got her from, and she said it was like walking into a house full of the undead. All the kids, just looking at you with those sullen eyes. Walking around outside, aimlessly. And it was in the city, you know, so the place was already a little grimy without the atmosphere if you know what I mean. Hmm? Oh, the McMullens? Don't tell me you don't know about them, now. Uh-huh, "in my own words," huh? Alright, then.

The McMullens lived right down the road, on that big apple orchard. I been workin' for 'em since I was eleven years old, pickin' apples and all sorts of other stuff for a kid's profit. It was me and a bunch of other sumbitches with nothin' else to do and nowhere else to go.

It's true that I talked to Mrs. a lot when I could; that's how I knew they were planning on adopting. Couldn't understand why, with the other heathens running around. But Mrs. McMullen always said she liked to think of herself as a humanitarian, you know? She wanted to care for people. She's a good lady, you know, deserves more than what she's been given. Sorry, off-topic. Where were we? Ah, yes, that day.

So the McMullens had gone down there to the city one day a couple months ago. Oh, alright, now. I know y'all are just doin' your job, and I respect that. But if you want the exact date, surely you could ask Mrs. McMullen? I see. Well, it's a shame y'all are like that, but I will oblige.

It would've been the fourteenth or fifteenth of July 1955, whichever one was on a Thursday. Just a regular hot-as-hell Alabama day. About an hour after the folks'd left, I was tendin' trees out in the orchard when I heard a scream coming from the house. There wasn't anybody else around who heard it, not that they'd care anyway, and so I started running toward it, even though I knew I wasn't allowed to step one foot inside that house. When I finally got there, I stayed outside the back door for a minute, daring myself to not be a bitch and go in, all the while knowin' that Mrs. McMullen'd kill me if I got dirt on her floor. I decided to take the risk and burst through the door.

Thankfully, there wasn't any maniacs in there or any of that. The only thing out of the ordinary was a broken vase on the floor, and sixteen-year-old Miss Betty McMullen, the eldest child, knelt down next to it, clutching her hand that was covered in blood.

"Aw hell, Miss Betty," I said. "Now, what'd you go and do that for?"

"Nothin', stupid," she said, like the charmer she is. "Just help me."

"Well, alrighty, Miss Betty, but your mamma's gonna pitch a fit if she finds me in here."

I walked over and helped her up, careful not to step on any broken glass. I took out the bandana that I keep in my pocket and started wrappin' it around her bleeding hand. I looked around at the floor around us.

"How'd you even manage to hurt yourself like that, anyway?" I asked. "Ain't the first time this week, neither. Remember the other day you missed a step and landed on your knee and cut it all up? Can't you go one day without an injury? I'm surprised you got any blood left."

She sighed and looked at her hand. "I remember, Tom, I was there." She winced as I was wrapping her hand. "I threw the vase, and when I went to pick up the pieces, I cut myself." I couldn't help it, I started laughing, and she hit me in the arm with her good hand. "Hey, you jerk! You better watch yourself, or I'll tell mamma you broke it!"

"Aw, c'mon, now, you know I was just foolin'." I got up and helped her off the floor. I kept her hands for a moment and then went back over to the door. "I do gotta get outta here, though. If I was you, I'd tell your mamma the little'n's did it. You know she'll forgive them."

"Yeah, you're sure right about that. Now get on outta here 'fore you get caught."

"I will," I said. "But you know, Miss Betty, if you ever need me, you know how to find me. And you, ma'am, are always welcome in my house."

She tried to look upset, but her smile gave her away. "You're a pervert, Tom Higgins!"

"Thank you, ma'am."

Was I flirting with Miss Betty? Sure, I was. Ain't no sense denyin' it. The girl was a fire lit under my behind, but hell, she's a beauty. Pretty red hair, and those glowing blue eyes, and the rest of her was never that bad, neither. I won't go into specifics because I'm a gentleman, but I'd've hated to be her daddy if you'll forgive me, gents. He had his hands full, that was for sure. I'd seen them boys come in from town with their fancy dress and their high-quality education come around askin' her questions. It seemed that was all they could do because Miss Betty wouldn't have nothin' to do with them. They just didn't have anything to impress her. To tell you the truth, up until recently, I thought she still had the hots for me, but I know now how silly it is to think that.

Now, if you're wondering why she broke the vase, I'll tell you. Miss Betty was angry because her mamma and daddy were getting another kid. Miss Betty sure didn't like that idea; you could bet your second serving on it. I learned later that they hadn't told her 'til that morning that they were even doing it. The younger ones didn't even know yet. It was supposed to be a surprise, but I didn't know if Mr. and Mrs. thought it was gonna be a good one or not, or whether they just didn't care. But Miss Betty wouldn't be letting 'em hear the last of it for a long while.

So I get out the front door just in time to hear the sound of hol-lerin' from the orchard. I was thinkin' of pretending not to hear it, but I'm too honest of a man to go running away from stuff, especially when I'm trusted by the family to watch out for the boys and make honest gentlemen out of them too. So I go running out behind the house and- what? 'What's this got to do with any-thing?' Now listen here, you asked me to tell you a story, and so you're gonna get a goddamn story. Now, where was I? Ah yes.

When I got around the house and just a little into the trees toward the noise, I could see Jimmy and Tuck around there just yellin' and screamin' at each other. Hmm? Oh, right, their full names are James Haroldson and Alan Tucker Holt. Oh, *now* you're interested. They was two big ol' workin' boys, and when I tell you those boys could find a disagreement over anything and every-thing, you better believe it. I'd had to break up a fight earlier that same week, dodgin' fists and all, over Jimmy stealin' a gardenin' hoe from Tuck. Even though Tuck had stolen it himself from old Mr. Jones down the road when he did work for him that last sum-mer. I broke up the fight and took the hoe back to Mr. Jones, who paid me five dollars just for bein' honest. That was supposed to be a life lesson for those boys, but it didn't do 'em any good appar-ently, because they just went back to fightin' the next day.

This time, they weren't fist fighting yet, but they looked well on their way to it. When I got to 'em, they were *this close* to each other, either one of 'em gettin' ready to snap. And the other boys were standing around 'em yellin' and carryin' on, ain't one of 'em get close enough to separate 'em. That was until they saw me comin' around, then they were sticking their arms out to take the boys' shoulders, pretending they weren't letting the fight go just to entertain themselves.

"Alright, quit foolin' now!" I told them. "Y'all got shit to do, don't ya?" Then I got in close range with Jim and Tuck, who still ain't hit each other, just there staring into each other's eyes, all precious. "And what the hell is the bother this time?" I asked them. "You stole his shit. He stole yours. I got half a mind to put names on everything, so you ain't got an excuse to fight no more."

"It ain't that, Tommy," Tuck said, not looking away from Jimmy while he was talking to me. "Jim here says I stole his lady friend."

"His what?" I asked, then looked at Jimmy, who still hadn't said a word. "You got a girl, Jim?" Not a word still. "Huh? Do ya?"

"No, Tommy, I don't," Jimmy said finally. "But I do got a sister, and this here sumbitch put his grubby hands on her."

The boys still lingering around were muttering to each other all the while, and the minute Jim said the word, "sister," they looked ready to jump in.

"You's one to talk about grubby hands, Jim. I ain't done nothing but tell her she looked nice," Tuck said. "I's bein' a gentleman, Tommy."

"You're full of shit, Tuck!" Jimmy yelled an inch from his face. "I saw the both of ya's behind the shed the other night from my winda. She's still young, and she don't want nothin' with you!"

"Ain't what she said the other night."

As you can imagine, it took off from there. They was back and forth and fighting with a rage that didn't have the energy to back it up, not after working most of the day. After a minute, me and a few other boys managed to get 'em away from each other. Tuck was on the ground, and I'd got Jimmy stood six or seven feet away from him, leanin' on an apple tree.

"That's enough now," I said to 'em, breathing hard and my arm achin' from a stray punch. "Y'all are lucky the folks are gone for the day and ain't seen ya messin' around. There's still work needs doin', and the way I figure it, y'all ain't gettin' paid to play fight all day long."

I glanced up at the house for a second, and I could just see Miss Betty looking out a second-story window, and when she saw me lookin', she disappeared.

I looked back down at the boys, most of 'em lookin' down all ashamed. Jimmy didn't look at me or anybody. Tuck was gettin' up from the ground, a bruise already formin' on the left side of his face.

"Go on, now," I said. "Get back to what you was doin'."

The boys all went their separate ways, not one lookin' at me. Jimmy went along with them, but Tuck stayed behind for a second.

"You got some nerve, Tuck," I said, once everyone else had gone. "You only went after that girl 'cause it was Jimmy's sister, didn't ya?"

"Tommy, I ain't go after no girl," he said. "We just got along, that's all."

"You could think again 'fore lyin' to me, Tuck," I said. "I worked with you for three years, now. I know what you're like."

Tuck stepped a little closer to me. "I could say something to you," he said real quiet, "about going after girls you shouldn't." He tilted his head toward the house, and I glanced for the quickest moment up at the window again.

I looked him in the eye and said seriously, "You know I ain't done nothin' I shouldn't. I say hello, she replies, that's it. Nothin' more to it."

He smirked at me a second, then walked away. I looked up at the window again, and Miss Betty was back, looking down at me. I knew I shouldn't be talkin' to her too much, or someone would start sayin' somethin'. I swear, I knew that then.

Now, y'all are sitting there noddin' off like ain't none of the stuff I told you was important. But it'll come back, I promise. But for now, the stuff you've been waitin' for. Because this is where the girl comes in.

Not twenty minutes after the fight, Mr. and Mrs. McMullen drove down the lane toward the house. I was around the front of the house pulling weeds when they pulled up. I saw the two of them get out of the car, and then Mr. McMullen opened the back door, and out of it came Miss Diamond. That's what I was supposed to call her, the same title of respect referrin' to all the family, and Miss Diamond was part of the family now.

She was a tiny little thing, wearin' a plain, dirty dress and one shoe. Lookin' a good bit different from her new parents, Mrs. with her dress and gloves and Mr. with his tie and hat. The child's wild curly brown hair was in tangles and knots on her head and in her face, so I could barely see her face at all except her eyes. She had these big light eyes that stared wide at everything around her. The thing that struck me was her left sleeve, which was hanging slack, empty. She was the poster child for a poor little orphan girl.

I had been staring for just a second too long and been caught by Mrs. McMullen, who waved over to me.

"Hey there, Tom!" she yelled over to me. "Wanna come here a second?"

I knew better than to say no, so I got up from weedin', wiped the dirt from my hands, and walked over to the three of them. What a sight I must have been, all sweat and dirt on that hot day. And what a sight they were to me, the perfect southern couple and their new baby urchin.

I greeted 'em, as I should when I reached 'em. "Howdy, there, Ma'am," I nodded to Mrs. McMullen, who smiled politely at me. "Hello, Sir," I nodded to Mr. McMullen, who looked at the dirt on my person and never in my eyes. "And you too, Ma'am." I looked down at Miss Diamond, and she looked back up at me with those big eyes and said nothin'. I had no idea what she might have been thinkin' 'cause she never gave anything away.

"Tom," the Mrs. said, "this is Diamond. We've just adopted her from a home in the city. She's coming to live with us, now."

Miss Diamond didn't move her gaze from me the whole time her new mamma was speakin'. I stayed lookin' at her, too.

"How d'ya do, Miss Diamond?" I asked.

She waited for a second and said, "Fine."

Mr. and Mrs. seemed surprised to hear her speak. I guess she hadn't been much of a talker on the drive home.

"Well then," Mrs. said, "We'll be getting her inside then. She's had a big day."

"She sure has," I said, still in a staring contest with the kid. "You're in good hands 'round here, Miss Diamond." I looked up and winked at Mrs. McMullen. Her husband had distracted himself with a small scratch on the car, and when Mrs. hurried Miss Diamond into the house with her, he followed, still saying nothing and never looking me in the eye.

Hmm? No, I don't know why he was like that. Kept to himself most times. No, I can promise you it wasn't about her. I'd been there for years, and he knew I wouldn't step out like that with Miss Betty. And in that specific situation, he was right. But you know that already, don't ya?

After that interaction, the way I understand it, Mrs. got the girl all cleaned up and introduced her to the siblin's: Miss Betty, Rodney who was twelve, the twins Imogen and Dolly, who were both nine, and little Billy, who was only seven. I was leavin' that afternoon just as it was happening, so I don't know what the introduction was like. All I knew was that things were gonna get a little more interestin' around the house.

* * *

~ 2 ~

A LONG OVERDUE VISIT

MONDAY, JULY 19, 1965. 09:16AM.

The tape cut out around there because as Tom Higgins finished the beginning of his story, the blood tests came back. And nobody felt the rest of the story was important. The case seemed pretty cut and dry without the extra time spent, one of the quickest closings all that year.

Detectives Isla Banks and Jerry Wild sat in an empty interrogation room in Montgomery, Alabama, looking between each other and the tape recorder on the table. They had just listened to an old testimony from a ten-year-old case, in which the detectives of Dothan asked a Mr. Tom Higgins to give his side of the story until they felt it was no longer necessary. When she'd read about the case the first time, Isla Banks had thought it unfair they never let him finish his story, whether the results seemed clear or not. But Lord, if it mattered to anyone important what *she* thought about it.

Isla Banks had only been a detective officially for seven months, finally breaking through the ranks after working as a traffic cop for three years prior. Even then, it had been a complete fluke that they'd even considered her, but given that she had effectively solved a case using only clues that were so public knowledge they were in the newspaper, of all things, it became hard to ignore her. After that, Banks had gotten lucky that the Montgomery police department finally decided she was worthy of their time. Now, she was a real detective who had just been assigned to a newly reopened case with her partner, Jerry Wild.

The two of them had been put together the first time because the Captain thought they would be a balanced match: different enough that if one hadn't thought of something during an investigation, chances are the other would have. It had worked well for them so far. Wild, whose surname was the antithesis to his personality, was quite different from Banks in style and almost everything else. While Banks was quick and passionate and excitable, Wild was stern and mellow and often not as interested. Wild was only three years older than Banks, but he was promoted almost straight out of the academy for his capability and had been a full-fledged detective for eight years. Wild had never been ignored or patronized, and while he liked his job, it was still just a job. When he left the building, he traded in the trials and tribulations of a detective's life for his outside passions, which mainly included driving his brand new '65 Chevy Impala home to kiss his wife and kids before sitting down to watch *Bonanza*.

Unlike Wild, Banks lived all the time in the detective mindset. She went into every day with the importance of her position at the forefront of her mind. She was a modern woman, determined to be flawless in her life and job, from her tortoiseshell cat-eye glasses to her Oxford shoes.

Despite their differences, the two got along just fine and sat in their respective silences without concern for the others. Even now, sitting at the interrogation table, Banks was whirling with thoughts and Wild was picking at his nails and staring at the wall, probably thinking but probably *not* about the case.

Just then, the door opened, and Sergeant Walter Nichols stepped into the room. A graying and thin Army veteran, he held himself high with his chin up and his chest out, as he had done for seemingly all his life. His was a way of perseverance and diligence, and complaints were never welcome. If the man had a catchphrase, it would have been, "I did not spend all that time shooting Nazi bastards between the eyes for y'all to bum around all day!" Banks had wondered if the man had ever shot *any* Nazi between the eyes, but it was never the right time to ask about it.

Banks and Wild stood for their superior, waiting for him to deliver the news they had been waiting for.

"Well, kids," he said, "They said y'all can go and talk to him."

Banks sighed and allowed herself to smile a little. Wild nodded slightly and did nothing else.

"I don't expect it to be easy, though," he continued. "He'll surely be wondering why you're back asking more questions. But we don't want him to know what we found yet. It could change the way he tells it, and we need to have all the details from the beginning."

"Yes, sir," Banks said, returning to seriosity. "After all this time, I hope he's eager to share the rest."

"I sure hope so," Sgt. Nichols said though he did not seem to be hopeful at all. "But don't get too excited about it. I granted this case to reopen for you, doll. I had to push a lot of people around to make this work. I don't know what you think's gonna come from it, but I hope for your sake it ain't nothing."

"Sarge, I have a good feeling about this," said Banks. "I have no question he was involved, but I have reason to believe there's more to it than that. And I think it might have something to do with the daughter that went missing, Diamond McMullen."

"Well, find out what you can," Sgt. Nichols turned to leave the room, then turned around again. "And before you go there, you should know Higgins is a talker. Once you get him goin', it'll be hard to shut him up."

"That's what I'm hoping for, Sarge," Banks said with a smile. The Sergeant left the room, and the two detectives looked at each other.

"Well," said Wild, speaking for the first time in hours, "you're finally gonna hear the rest of the story."

"Oh, it's not about that, Wild," Banks said, still smiling despite herself. "I really think there's more to this than anyone was willing to look into last time. I've got a feeling."

"Well, we know what happens when you have a feeling," said Wild.

TUESDAY, JULY 20, 1965. 07:56 AM.

"Why couldn't we do a case a little closer by?" Wild asked.

The two of them had gotten up at six in the morning the next day and driven for two hours in Wild's Impala from Montgomery to a town called Dothan, Alabama, because their new friend and person of interest was staying in the penitentiary there.

"Oh, it's not even that far," Banks said, as Wild carefully pulled into a parking space. "And aren't you ready for a story?" Wild said nothing. "Or at least getting away from Jefferson for the day?"

Wild looked over at her and allowed a small smile. Detective Jefferson was a chatty lady who always asked about everyone's day and told them about hers, which would have been nice for everyone but Jerry Wild.

"Yeah, alright," he said, opening his door. "Let's get this over with."

Wild and Banks were shown into the dimly lit cells right away, which were mostly empty at this time of day. The penitentiary had said that they didn't have any private accommodations to offer this conversation. Still, Banks didn't want too many people around them, in case a personal matter or embarrassing subject compromised how open Higgins was willing to be. The correctional officers told Banks and Wild that they would have about an hour with Higgins while the other inmates were eating their breakfast and doing various supervised work around the prison. Banks didn't like working on a crunch but took what they gave her, knowing from experience that there was no use causing a fuss that would not be rewarded.

The subject of their visitation was already waiting for them in his cell. When she saw him, Banks felt like she was looking at a legend. She'd seen his mugshot so many times, looking through his file and all the case information she could get her hands on. It almost didn't seem like he should be real.

He was a little worse for wear, that was for sure. He'd grown his dark hair out, and a considerable amount of facial hair had appeared since his arrest ten years before. He had probably been able to shave it, and maybe he did every so often, but it seemed he didn't care much about how he looked. Even underneath his rugged appearance, though shadowy in spots, his face was still young, as he was only twenty-seven years old, only a year younger than Banks herself. He had his striped prison uniform on, and he sat on his bed with his hands folded in his lap while he waited for the detectives. When he looked up and saw them, he smiled just a little, and his blue eyes twinkled in a ray of light coming in through a grated window in the concrete wall. It wasn't a crazy smile, or even over-eager, just a polite smile of greeting, as though he had seen a friend from across the street.

Banks resisted the urge to smile back at him, even though she really wanted to, not only because of her excitement at finally getting a chance at this case but also because he just seemed like someone to which it was okay to smile back. He had a friendly face. But she knew better than to go compromising her professionalism and tried her best to remind herself why Higgins was in that cell in the first place.

The guard opened the cell door for Wild and Banks to go in and sit where they had put two chairs for them opposite Higgins' bed. They sat and waited as the guard closed the door behind them, then went to his post at the end of the hall, having assured them he was always waiting and listening if they needed him. Not a second had passed after the guard leaving that Higgins said his first words to them. He was so quick to break the quiet they had been hearing; it almost made the two detectives jump.

"Gotta be honest," he said, with the same voice they'd heard on the tape, if just the slightest touch lower, "not many around here're too excited to have cops come and talk to 'em. But it sure has been a long time since anyone's come callin' on me, so can't say I'm complainin'."

"I'm sure it has been a while," Banks said to him, still resisting the urge to smile, which was becoming more difficult by the minute as Higgins' kind eyes bore into her. *Remember, Isla,* she thought to herself. *Remember how he got here.*

"Tom Higgins," she began, "My name is Detective Banks, and this is Detective Wild." She gestured toward her partner, who nodded but said nothing, as was his usual. "We're here to ask you about your case. We want to get the whole story if you don't mind."

When she said this, she noticed Wild look over to her for a moment. *Here we go,* her partner was probably thinking. She did not move her eyes from Higgins but turned her chin in Wild's direction as if to say, *deal with it.*

Higgins didn't seem to notice this small exchange. He just smiled again and said, "Well, I think it's about time. Where should I begin?"

~ 3 ~

NEW BEGINNINGS

"You left off last time with the girl's arrival," Banks prompted Higgins, with her notepad on her lap, ready for notes. "You had just met her for the first time, and you said things were going to get, 'interesting.' How about you take off from there?"

Higgins smiled at her introduction and looked down at the floor, then up at the wall. He looked pensive and glassy, as he let himself walk down a road he hadn't seen in years.

"Yeah, well, 'interestin'' would cover it, I'd say," he said, still not looking them in the eye. "Let's see..."

* * *

Well, things went about as well as you'd think, I guess. I'm sure you already know the oldest McMullen child, Miss Betty, wasn't happy about the situation, but the other kids had their own ways of letting everyone know they weren't fans of it, neither. They wouldn't say it in front of their mamma, no sir, but they sure gave that little'n a hard time.

I suppose the first time I saw any of 'em in the act was about three days later. I was out in the orchard doin' my thing around noon time, and I heard the sound of little voices around. I looked up towards the house, and right there at the edge of the rows was the twins, Dolly and Imogen, although most called Imogen, "Idgie," for short, and little Billy was runnin' around 'em. There with Miss Idgie and Miss Dolly was Miss Diamond, sat on the ground with her arm behind her, looking up at the two of them, staring back down at her.

Now, most wouldn't think nothin' of it, and it wasn't my place to be in anyone's business, but you couldn't help but wanna look after Miss Diamond. Not only did she have the one arm, but she was just so small. She was a whole four years older than the twins, but she didn't have a single pound or inch on either of 'em. And the way she was leaning back then, I didn't have to have looked a second earlier to know that them girls was takin' advantage of her petiteness and had pushed her over. And if that wasn't enough, as I was watchin', Miss Diamond tried gettin' herself off the ground, which she *could do,* but it sure wasn't graceful, weak legs wobblin' and all. And when she was almost all the way up, Miss Idgie went and pushed her back down, and she fell pretty hard.

Now things like this would happen all the time with them ankle-biters runnin' around. I'd have to keep Billy from throwin' himself off stuff most days, he was just the most curious kid you ever met. He'd always be askin' all the boys out there what stuff was, and just when we started wonderin' what he was doin' out there, his mamma would yell for him, silly kid.

I didn't really have the authority to discipline 'em, but since I was older, they usually'd respect me enough to stop. So I went up the row to 'em this time to get 'em to leave'r alone.

"Hey now," I said. "Whatcha gon' do that for?"

The twins looked up at me all eyes, waitin' to get shouted at. That's the thing about kids, they know it's wrong, what they're doin', don't mean they're not gonna do it if they want to. They don't have enough maturity yet to do the right thing because its right, not just 'cause they'll get yelled at. Miss Diamond looked up at me, too. She had a little somethin' different sittin' in her eyes. Where there was shame in Miss Idgie and Miss Dolly's eyes, the only thing I saw in Miss Diamond's was surprise and curiosity. I know now it's because she was used to handlin' things herself. She wasn't used to being helped.

"We didn't do nothin'," Miss Idgie said. "She fell down."

"Now, Miss Idgie," I said. "You know well I just saw you push her down. You know it ain't nice to go doing stuff like that. Miss Diamond is only little, but it don't mean you should push her around, do it?"

They put their heads down, pretendin' to be disappointed in themselves. Only thing they was disappointed about was gettin' caught.

"No, it don't," they both said back to me.

"Alright, go on and play now," I said, and the twins went off running somewhere else. I turned to Miss Diamond and put my hand out to help her up. She looked at me a second before takin' it. When I tell you I was liftin' her whole weight to get her up, and you'd've thought it was like liftin' a puppy dog.

Miss Diamond's new blue dress her mamma had put her in was covered in dirt already from fallin'. One of her socks was up and one was down, and her wild hair was done up, but a lot of it couldn't be held in place no matter what her mamma had done. She wasn't as desperate-lookin' as she had been before, but she was still just a little off. She looked up at me, and I don't know if she was waiting for me to speak or what she was doing, but there was a moment we just looked at each other 'fore I decided maybe I should say somethin'.

"They was just foolin', Miss Diamond," I said. "They ain't used to havin' you around, yet. They'll warm up to ya, don't you worry."

She looked down at herself, then she said, "They pushed me because they don't like me. They think I'm weird for havin' one arm."

I wasn't sure what to say to that. I knew it was probably true, but I didn't wanna fuel that fire too much.

"Well," I said, "can't say they've probably seen anybody with one arm before. They's only young. It's just somethin' they'll be havin' to learn." I went to touch her on the shoulder, 'cause it felt like the right time for somethin' like that. But this girl wasn't sociable like that, so I decided not to, "But if anybody tries somethin' like that again, you know I'll be around to help if ya need me."

This time she didn't miss a beat when she said, "I won't need you. I can take care of myself."

I was a little took back by that. I liked that she was a tough talker like she was, so I smiled at her and said, "I bet you can. But I ain't like the folks you're used to dealin' with. You can call on me if you need anything at all."

She looked like she was ready to argue, but she seemed to accept it.

"Okay," she said.

I said, "You know sometimes a polite young lady like you might say, 'Thank you.'"

She just blinked and said, "Get lost."

That was my first real interaction beyond meetin' her that I'd had. I didn't think anything of it, I was just bein' friendly, like I tried to be with all the family. After that I went back to workin', then when sunset came around and I was walking up the rows to get goin', Miss Betty jumped out at me from behind one of the trees.

"Jesus, Miss Betty!" I said. "What are you doin' there? Gonna give me a heart attack!"

She was just laughing. She had a bandage around her hand where she'd cut herself, but otherwise was happy and well. I loved the way she was smilin'.

"I was waitin' to talk to you," she said. "I knew there wouldn't be anyone out here this time of night."

I said, "Oh, so you're tryin' to get me alone, are you?"

She just looked at me with that know-it-all look on her face. "I was just tryin' to tell you it was real sweet of you, going to help Diamond earlier."

"Warmed up to her, have ya?" I asked.

"Not quite," she said. "But it's not like it's her fault. She didn't ask to be adopted by my parents, to a family with more than enough kids already that I have to look after most of the time. And it's not fair, her bein' crippled like that."

"I'm sure she'd say so," I said, laughin' at how Miss Betty looked like she had given up.

"Well, you know what I mean," she said. "Mamma knew I couldn't be too upset because of a poor little girl with one arm. She knows I don't like the idea, and that it would be easier for me to care about a child like that."

"Oh, so you care, now, huh?" I asked, poking at her shoulder.

"Oh, well maybe I do," she said, smilin'. "She ain't hurtin' anybody, I guess. I wish the twins would leave her alone. I was just about to come outside and give them hell before I saw you there."

We'd been slowly movin' closer to each other all the time. I was lookin' down into her eyes when I said, "What can I say, Miss Betty? I *am* a gentleman, after all."

"You sure are, Tom Higgins," she said, and she put her hand on my arm. "You got kindness. Ain't too many of the other boys 'round here care like you do."

They sure didn't, neither. The other boys was there for work and that was it. Ain't no shame in that, of course, but I was lookin' for a little somethin' more out of life.

Then, I think she realized how close we were gettin', 'cause she took her hand off my arm and turned to start walkin' back toward the house. The sun was goin' down and they's about ready to have some supper. Didn't want her daddy askin' her too many questions 'bout where she been, even though ain't no one was doin' a thing wrong.

"You don't have to run away from me, Betty," I said, biting my lip and takin' a chance. "You ain't got a thing to worry about with me."

She turned around to look at me and gave a little smile.

"I know, Tom," she said. "It ain't you I'm worried about."

I can't say I ever thought me and Betty was gonna go too far, but I'd be a damn liar if I said it wasn't what I wanted. I didn't have all that privileged an upbringing, as I'm sure you know. It would have been nice to have someone with a little bit o' money and a family around who gave a damn.

But that wasn't the big thing. You gotta understand, I never had any big ambitions. There wasn't anywhere I needed to get to, so there wasn't any ladder to climb, steppin' on people all the way. Any kind of physical things that came along were only ever the icin' on the cake. I wanted to be with Betty because she was kind. She was a good girl, a pretty one, too. She didn't see me for what I was: a poor ol' sumbitch kid who had nothin' and nobody, who was gonna labor 'til the day he was dead and gone, because ain't nothin' else he knew how to do. Betty was a light at the end of a tunnel I hadn't known I was in.

Look at me, now. See what that girl's done to me? I ain't even callin' her, 'Miss,' no more. She's got me forgettin' myself, that's for sure, but I guess I haven't forgotten her as much as I thought I had. I've sure done her wrong, don't y'all know it? She'll never forgive me.

* * *

Banks tried hard not to show any pity forming beneath the surface as Higgins stopped speaking and looked down again. She never had a problem with sympathy in her work, not ever. But there was something about this man that made it so difficult to stay impartial.

That's probably how he managed to escape execution, she thought. She had wondered about that, too, since reading the case file the first time. In the state of Alabama the way it was in 1955, and *still* was now in 1965, a man who confessed to murdering two men, as well as being involved in an adulterous affair directly related to one of the victims, was a sure shot for the chair. Folks around there never liked things out of the ordinary and were ready to stamp out any threat to any man's standard and boring life, as was his right.

The three of them sat in silence for just a moment. Some inmates were being returned to their cells one by one, and at the moment no one spoke, they could hear footsteps above them and muffled voices from here and there.

Banks had let her mind wander thinking about what Higgins had talked about, so Wild took liberty in speaking for the first time since they'd arrived.

"So, the other children didn't like this Diamond girl," he said. "And that's why she ran away?"

Higgins shot back down to Earth and looked at Wild as if he had just noticed he was there. "Oh, so he *can* talk?" He said, a smile spreading across his bearded face as he looked from Wild to Banks. "I's worried it was just gonna be us talkin'."

There it is again, she thought. *That contagious smile. Can this man let me be a cold cop for once?*

"I think," Banks said, bringing herself back into the zone, "what my partner is trying to ask is: how do these events relate to the crime itself? As much as you cared about Betty McMullen, I'm not sure what that has to do with what we're asking for."

Higgins' content face hadn't moved the entire time Banks had been speaking. He listened politely and spoke in the same manner.

"Well, now, Miss Detective," he said, still smiling, "I thought y'all was wantin' the *whole* story. Ain't that what you said? And besides, every 'event' I've told ya about is a rung on the ladder. Every single one is just as important to the story as the last. Don't wanna go slippin' now, do ya?"

Banks could feel Wild begin to lose any interest he'd had in this interview and knew she should wrap it up fairly soon, however interested *she* still was.

"Okay," she said, compromising her traditional to-the-point method in an attempt to collect anything Higgins was willing to give. "So, how do these interactions with Diamond and Betty McMullen tie into the story, then?"

"Well," Higgins said, "Miss Betty was the reason I got so friendly with Miss Diamond. Remember she told me how much she liked that I was friendly with the kid, helpin' her out and all. 'Spose you could say I's tryin' to impress Miss Betty by being kind. Ain't nothin' wrong with that, after all."

"So, was Diamond there that night?" Banks asked, feeling like she'd hit something finally. "You're telling us about becoming friends with her because she was around the scene of the crime?"

Higgins, while continuing to smile, took just a moment longer to respond than was his usual.

"No," he said, and Banks noticed Wild start to tap his foot softly. "No, she wasn't there. Thank God, too. Somethin' like that ain't no place for a child. I'd never have wanted her to see that."

The smile that stayed on Higgins' face while referring for the first time to the night he murdered two people started to seem a little forced, and it was something only someone as shrewd and determined as Isla Banks would have noticed.

"Mr. Higgins," Banks said softly, wanting, for some reason, not to press too hard. As if a confessed murder is a sensitive subject everyone experiences. "That night. The night of the murders. Was anyone else there with you and the victims?"

Higgins seemed somehow more relaxed when he answered. "No," he said. "Just me and them."

Banks felt her shoulders slump involuntarily. She had not realized how tightly she'd been holding herself. More inmates were entering the cell block, signaling that she had run out of time. Higgins noticed her disappointment and let his expression slacken.

"Detective," he said to her, no longer worrying about addressing Wild, who was looking around aimlessly, "Don't get me wrong, here. I've enjoyed the company this mornin', but my case has been settled for ten years. I gotta wonder what it is we're doin' here."

Banks looked into this man's eyes and had no wish to lie to him, but her training and professional drive overcame her wish to be honest with this seemingly honest man. This honest, murdering, adulterous man.

"It's mostly a passion project, truly," she began. "I've wanted to hear more about this story since I read the case file a few years back. That, and," Banks tried to think quickly. She had prepared her traditional, *That's classified, and I don't have to explain anything to you,* response in case he asked why, but it didn't feel right anymore. It just wasn't the right mood.

"And I probably shouldn't tell you this, but I want to be honest with you..." Banks lent in a bit, and Higgins followed her lead and lent in himself, looking around as he did so. Wild looked to her, showing his first bit of concern, but letting her do whatever it was she was doing.

"There was an issue with a case just a month ago. Somebody over in Birmingham who'd done something real bad walked with no charge because the officers working the case messed around with the evidence files. So the State of Alabama has got us going around double-checking stories from people still living, so they cover their bases before someone finds anything fishy." Banks looked around again at the inmates filing in and sat back up, indicating the end of the private information. "This case is only my assignment. My partner's mostly here for backup; the Sergeant wasn't comfortable with sending me into a men's prison all alone."

She glanced over at Wild and elbowed him in a friendly way, trying to make it seem like they'd joked about it before. Though not at all theatrical, Wild did a decent job in returning the favor, smiling just a little and nodding in affirmation. He seemed relieved that he knew what she was doing now.

Higgins considered this and seemed to accept it as the truth. His smile returned to his face.

"Well," he said, almost laughing, "I'd hate to be the sumbitches that got all messed up with the state, that's for damn sure." He looked around at the increasingly populated cell block and sighed. "I suppose it's probably time for y'all to bug out?"

"Yes," Wild said, a little too eager. He looked between Higgins and Banks and cleared his throat. "Um, yes. That was our slot, and we have other cases to look into today. Right, Banks?"

"We sure do," she responded, trying not to be too animated about it. "Thank you for talking to us, Mr. Higgins."

"Oh, anytime," he said, still smiling but looking a little deflated. "Was that all you needed?"

"Oh, no!" Banks said, a little too excited, as she stood up. Wild had already crossed to the door and was waving down the guard. When Banks said this, he looked back at her with slightly raised eyebrows.

"No," she said, calmer this time. "I've got lots of holes I still need you to fill. We want this case as complete and *safe* as possible. And besides, this is also a passion project, remember? Oh, I'll be back for more."

Higgins perked up, and there was a twinkle in his eye again. "Well, I'll be happy to see ya when you come back. Always a pleasure to see a friendly face around here, and a pretty one, too, if you'll forgive me, Detective." He winked at her then, and she didn't like the way she liked it.

"I'll see you next time, Mr. Higgins," she said, allowing a natural smile for the first time, which felt terrific. The guard had come around, and Wild had already walked out of the cell and was walking toward the block door. Banks started walking out, too. Then she remembered something she'd written down in her notes that morning and turned around in the doorway to look back at Higgins.

"Mr. Higgins," she said, trying to organize her thoughts, "I almost forgot. Ten years ago, when interrogated you the first time, you spoke about two boys, Jimmy and...?"

"Tuck," Higgins provided, his ever-present smile fading just a bit.

"Tuck," Banks confirmed. "You spoke about those two boys fighting and that it would be important leading up to what happened the night you were arrested. How do *they* play into the story?"

"Well, now," he teased. "You'll just have to wait 'til next time."

09:14 AM.

"Well, that was a bust."

Banks turned her head towards Wild in the driver's seat, her eyebrows furrowed together.

"What do you mean?" She asked.

Wild raised his own eyebrows and let out the beginning of a laugh. "We got nothing from that! No new clues, no leads, nothing even remotely related to the murders. Just a man telling stories like he's havin' a campfire."

Banks faced forward and sighed.

"I'll allow you that the story was long-winded," she said, "but a bust it was not."

"Oh, don't tell me," Wild said, in that same stern tone he always used. "Banks, you're good. In fact, you're better than good. But even *you* can't have possibly gotten something from *that*."

Banks took in the compliment and used it to fuel her following statement.

"Just the beginnings of something, really," she said, staring out at the hot Alabama asphalt in front of them. "No, we didn't get anything concrete for the case. But why would he spend so much time building that girl into a story, just to say she wasn't involved at all at the end? Did you see the way he looked when I asked about it? It was like he'd been caught in the act like he said something he definitely shouldn't and didn't realize until it was too late.

"And did you notice how I phrased the question?" Banks flipped back in her notebook excitedly. "'Was *anyone else* there with you and *the victims?*' And then he said, 'No, just me and *them.*' Do you get it?"

Wild tried to make it seem like he did get it but quickly changed his mind and said, "No?"

"Wild!" She exclaimed, amused. "Think about it! Maybe it was just him and the victims, but what if there were more victims than the two we know of already?"

Wild finally managed to jump on Banks' train of thought. "You think he killed the girl, too?"

"It's possible," Banks said, slumping back in her chair, having run out of her short burst of steam. "That being said, it doesn't make perfect sense. He would have had to hide her body really well for them never to find her, but why the effort with her and not the others? I can understand the theatrics in the story, focusing on her in memoriam and regret, or maybe later explaining how he came to hate her? Or maybe she'd witnessed something she wasn't supposed to? That would make sense with the whole, 'I'd never have wanted her to see that,' which is a sentence that still makes sense if she *had* seen it. Maybe he hid her and not them because he felt guilty for killing a child? He would have certainly gotten the chair if she was included in the charges. Still, would an eighteen-year-old farmhand know enough about the law to know the differences in murder charges in Alabama, especially if it was a crime of passion and not at all premeditated? And as if that weren't enough, there is the small issue of the murder weapon—"

"Goodness gracious," Wild said, breaking her stream of ponderance, "you did get on to something, didn't you? Could be, you know. Could be."

"I'm glad you think so, Wild," Banks said, "because even given the possibilities of the theory, there's still something bothering me."

"What's that?" Wild asked.

"Well," she turned a little toward him but looked past him and out his window as she let out her thoughts. "I've been doing this for just a little while. But I've seen a lot of people in that time. Disregarding that, you've been doing this for much longer than me and seen countless more."

Wild furrowed his eyebrows a little. "What're you getting at, Banks?"

"Well, I can only speak for myself," she said. "But Tom Higgins doesn't seem like a murderer to me."

~ 4 ~

STICKS AND STONES

WEDNESDAY, JULY 21. 1965. 09:27 AM.

"But it's only been a day!"

Sgt. Nichols had called Banks and Wild into his office the day after their first visit with Higgins. Banks knew this wouldn't be good, but she had hoped that, for once, they would let her work for a little while before calling in questioning. She couldn't help but think about how this situation would play out if this case had been Wild's idea instead of hers.

We'd be out there on company time, she thought, *looking around for all the details, talking to witnesses, and exploring anything that looked like a lead. We wouldn't have to worry about whether what we were doing would beg questions from the higher-ups because they would trust Wild's judgment as an experienced detective and as a man. We certainly wouldn't be sitting here in the Sergeant's office, listening to him question my judgment and telling us the case is on the verge of being pulled after a single day.*

"Sir," Banks said, reeling in her emotions after having what the Sergeant would consider a "hysterical" response, "It has only been a day since we started talking to Higgins. We're in the beginning stages, but we have a testimony to play with. It's just a matter of getting it organized and turning it into something."

Nichols was looking across his desk at Banks without feeling, as it wasn't in his character. At least now, he didn't look as personally insulted as he had when Banks had spoken the first time because it was unacceptable that *she*, of all people, should question *him*, though *he* would never hesitate to question *her*.

Wild, though usually stoic and silent during these discussions, attempted to come to Banks' rescue. "Sarge," he said, and the Sergeant turned his head to look at him, "We *have* only just started. Banks is a good detective, sir, and if she believes there's more to be had in this case, I trust her judgment."

It was a nice sentiment, and Banks appreciated it. Unfortunately, however, it just wasn't good enough.

"Listen here, kids," the Sergeant said, taking off the reading glasses he'd been wearing and beginning to clean them with a cloth, as an excuse not to look in their eyes, "Cap feels like there are other things y'all should be doin,' things in the present. We got lots of things to occupy you, Banks. There's a missin' old lady case just came in."

Banks held back the wish to roll her eyes. The last time there was a missing elderly person, they had just been down at the lodge playing bingo like they did every Tuesday, and their spouse had forgotten what day it was and reported them missing. It was the most ridiculous and unsatisfying waste of time that Banks remembered experiencing.

"With all due respect, Sarge," Banks said, "a case like that is more fitted for one of the others. I think I'm capable of handling a bigger case than that."

The Sergeant looked up from his cleaning and into her eyes, and Banks imagined an eggshell breaking, knowing immediately that she had overstepped.

"Is that right?" He asked, with wide, mocking eyes as he put his reading glasses back on. "Well, if you're so good, maybe *you* can take this Higgins thing, for as long as it's not pulled, *on your own*."

"Sir?" Wild asked with the slightest questioning uplift in tone, sitting up in his chair and looking between the Sergeant and Banks, while Banks kept her eyes on the floor.

"Wild, why don't you take that Haroldson case?" The Sergeant asked.

"The one downtown?" Wild asked, with a touch of worry, enough of a change in his flat tone that Banks looked up from the floor at him, and she was shocked to see a bead of sweat forming on his forehead.

However shrewd of Banks' emotional changes, the Sergeant did not seem to notice the difference in Wild's mood at all. "That's the one, detective. That upset with them negroes down there. You know how they are."

Banks held her tongue so hard she thought she'd bite the damn thing off. She wasn't one for the views of the majority of her colleagues, and she had never been shy about providing a debate on the subject. But that subject had been so tense this year, more than ever, and she had only narrowly dodged what could have been a very real bullet when she had taken some unexplained time off in March. She said she'd been "traveling out of town," which wasn't too far off the truth, except she hadn't been visiting family over in Louisiana like she said she had been. Instead, she'd been tending to some personal beliefs over in Selma. Even as buried in the crowd as she had made herself, it was a miracle that the wrong people hadn't recognized her. If any person in the station caught wind of her actual whereabouts at that time, she would have been more than fired; they would make sure she would never do police work ever again.

She sat in the uncomfortable chair in the Sergeant's office, hoping the tightness in her form wasn't too apparent and praying that the Sergeant would take mercy on the subject for once, but he tortured her further.

"President Johnson's gone all soft on 'em," he said, still only speaking to Wild as though Banks was not there at all. "Damn coward. And now they're using it as an excuse to go hog wild. I'll tell you what, those downtowners ain't good for nothin' but causin' trouble. Stupid ni—"

Banks flinched involuntarily, and immediately dread filled her. The Sergeant noticed.

"Are you alright there, Detective?" He asked her. Wild glanced over to her. His face was indifferent, but his energy, which Banks had become adept at deciphering, was that of concern.

"I'm fine, sir," Banks said, sitting up and taking a deep breath. "Just a chill. So, am I allowed to continue this case? I understand I'll be alone."

The Sergeant seemed disappointed that he hadn't dampened her spirits enough for her to let this go, but he rolled his eyes and said, "Sure, Detective. But remember that I'm putting my neck on the line for you." He wasn't. "And not to mention we're putting expenses into this." They weren't. "I hope you can make something out of it." He didn't.

"Thank you, sir," Banks said. "I will."

10:02 AM.

Wild and Banks went out to Wild's Impala, as they usually did after a conversation with the Sergeant, to collect their thoughts and discuss. A car conversation was one of their unspoken traditions, along with going to Easy's Bar downtown when they completed a case to celebrate.

The second they closed the car doors, Wild surprised everyone involved by being the first to speak.

"I have never seen him try and pull something so fast before," he said.

Banks felt like she could explode. "He's full of shit."

"Now, you know it's not personal, Isla," Wild addressed her by her first name, which was a signal he used to let her know that he was speaking to her as a friend instead of a coworker. "They just have their reservations about things. Sometimes what you want isn't what they think is right, and they use their authority to get rid of it. That's just the way it goes sometimes."

Banks knew that Wild's had good intentions. She knew he was honest and believed that this was just another example of a demanding boss, as bosses often are. But she also had a hard time believing that that was the full extent of the reason why this case, *her* case, was suddenly not good enough to consider fooling with.

"Personal or not," she said, "you know this wouldn't be so hard if it were your case."

Wild sighed and looked forward. "The Sarge is of an older crowd," he said. "There's not much you can do to change his mind once he's set on something. But sometimes, you just gotta take what you're given. Look at it this way: at least for now, you still have the case."

"*For now*," she repeated, "what good is *for now* if I might not have enough to satisfy them tomorrow or the next day, and they don't think I'm good enough to deliver, so they cut the case before I can even start thinking? And now I have to do it alone! He's crippling me, Jerry!"

Wild swallowed. "Yeah, no kidding," he said. "Now he's got me on the Haroldson case, and I..." He trailed off. His tone had been the same as always, but when Banks looked over at him, she noticed a shine in his eyes.

"Hey, you alright?" She asked softly, placing her hand gently on his right arm.

He kept his eyes forward. "I read about it the other day. This young colored boy. They're saying he pushed somebody, a white man, off the Pettus Bridge a week ago. The kid said he saw the man jump, but the family wants him put to death, 'for his crimes.'" He glanced in her direction, though still not looking her in the eye. "He's just a kid, Banks. No more'n seventeen. It don't feel right. I'm tellin' ya."

Wild glanced at her, then turned back forward, took a pause, and continued speaking.

"I know where you were in March, Banks." She held her breath as he spoke, the both of them sitting very still. "You know I'm no hippie; I'm not like that. I can't go around speaking out about stuff like that; It just ain't how I do things."

Banks sat there in silence, listening to him speak. Where was this going? Surely if he was going to say something about her to Sgt. Nichols or the Captain, he would have done so already, so why bring it up now?

"Wild, I..." she began.

"Hold on, now," he said, "I'm not finished. I don't go around like that; I'm not the kind of guy to cause an upset about something. But it doesn't mean I don't think about some things different than the other men in there." He jerked his head softly to the right, where the station was sitting. "To be honest, I'm just scared stiff about how they're gonna try to spin this case. I don't know if I have the power to stop them from doin' it, either."

Banks let herself relax, and a small smile of relief appeared on her face. "Wild, I know you'll try your best to do the right thing," she said. "Just remember: if you let them run it into the ground, you'll be feeling it for much longer than you'll be suffering from their opinions. You can bet on that."

Wild looked over and met her gaze. "I know," he said.

They sat in silence for a moment longer, taking in the conversation they had just had. It should not have felt like such a trial to do the right thing, especially as an officer of the law. Banks and Wild both knew this in their own ways.

Wanting to change the subject, Wild said, "So, are you gonna be okay doing this case on your own? As long as you have it, I mean?"

"I'll be fine," Banks said, somehow feeling like her determined energy had been renewed.

FRIDAY, JULY 23, 1965. 07:59 AM.

Banks was almost disappointed that she was looking forward to the two-hour trip to Dothan compared to the rest of her job. Being a detective is more than just solving cases and putting bad guys behind bars; there was always a massive pile of paperwork to be done. While Banks usually didn't mind the busy work, working a good case like this made her antsy, and all she wanted to do was get back on the clue trail, however minuscule it often was at this stage of the investigation.

It had been almost a week since the first time she had been to the penitentiary, and this time she asked for private accommodations beforehand. Even though she and Wild had been told last time that there were no such accommodations to be had, she would be allowed an empty solitary confinement cell to use this time. After telling the officer on the phone that she would be coming alone this time and that she was nervous about the idea of being in a cell block of a men's prison without any backup, they reluctantly agreed to allow her to use a solitary confinement cell to interview Higgins. Banks hated the idea of using her womanhood as an ailment that required remedy. But she knew that if it got her what she needed, it was a necessary sacrifice, however much it damaged her pride.

The same guard showed Banks down a different corridor upon her arrival, a briefcase bag slung over her shoulder, so she knew they must have made good on their promise. They reached a door about halfway down the hall, and the guard stopped before letting her inside.

"If you wish for me to stay outside," he said. "I'll have to cuff him."

Banks blinked. For a moment, she couldn't understand why before remembering that the man she had listened to talk about farm work and young love would be considered a danger.

"Yes," she said, "of course. Well, I suppose you should cuff him, then."

"Yes, ma'am," he said. It was somewhat refreshing that this guard didn't question her request. She often forgot that it was possible to ask for something and receive it without a fuss.

The guard opened the door to the cell, and they had set up a table and two chairs in the grim, fluorescently lit room. Sitting at the chair facing toward the door was Tom Higgins, waiting patiently for his visitor. Banks noticed that, while he still kept his long hair on his head and face, he didn't look quite as rugged as he had before. When she walked in, he gave her his charming smile again, quietly cooperated as the guard cuffed him, and waited as Banks sat down and the guard left, closing the door behind him.

"Nice to see you again, Detective," Higgins said, as though greeting an old friend.

"And you, Mr. Higgins," she said. For some feeling, she was feeling calmer here, in a solitary confinement cell with a convicted killer, than she had been feeling earlier in the week sitting in the Sergeant's office. She took her notepad and pen out of her bag and set them on her lap, relaxing in her seat and ready to listen.

"I know you're tryna be all formal," he said, "but you *can* call me Tom if you wanna."

Banks felt that sneaking sympathy come back. Her first thought should have been to stick to her senses, stay professional. But her actual first thought was that she felt sorry that Higgins probably hadn't had any visitors of any kind in a long time if he had ever had any. Did anyone call him 'Tom' here? If not, how long had it been since he had heard his first name regularly?

"Okay," she decided. "Tom, then."

"What about you, Detective?" he asked, teasing. "Can I call you by *your* first name?"

She smiled back at him without a second thought. "I think let's stick to, 'Detective,' for now, Tom."

Tom Higgins' smile was like the sun emerging after a storm.

"Can I at least ask you some questions' fore you start askin' me some?" He prodded.

Banks sighed and rolled her eyes. She shifted in her chair and put her hands in her lap, forgetting her notes for a moment. "Alright then," she said. "What do you wanna know?"

Tom sat back in his chair, cuffed hands outstretched and resting on the table between them. His face was smug but not sleazy. Proud, but not arrogant. Banks felt somewhat warm but chose to attribute the feeling to southern summer weather and not the man before her.

"What kind of music do you like, Detective?" He asked her, with a cheerful look in his eyes.

Banks was not exceptionally prepared for this question. She took a moment to think while Tom laughed at her indecision.

"I'm sorry," he said, "I thought it was gonna be easy."

"Well, I like a lot of music," Banks said, now laughing along with him. "And it's not all the same kind either. I listen to a lot of folksy stuff nowadays. Bob Dylan, Simon and Garfunkel, I like the Byrds. I like a lot of British bands, too. The Beatles, of course, the Stones..."

"Whoa, hold on now," Tom said, laughing more and waving his fingers from the table for her to stop. "I sure have been in here a long time because I didn't recognize a thing you just said."

Banks put a palm to her head, embarrassed for having forgotten. Tom would not have had much access to current music unless a guard played anything on the radio for the inmates, which she doubted was a frequent occurrence. She attempted to tune the conversation a little closer to Tom's wheelhouse.

"Well," she said to a still, very smiley Tom, "I always liked Sinatra."

"Now, there's a name I recognize!" Tom said, clearly appreciative to be considered. "Goodness, I never knew a woman in my life who didn't like Sinatra. I always liked that 'world on a string' song. Yeah, good ol' Frank. He still singin'?"

"Oh, sure!" Banks said. "He put out a record just earlier this year singin' that song, 'Luck Be a Lady,' from the musical Guys and Dolls if you know it. Oh, I don't see him stopping anytime soon."

"I think I might," Tom said, and he looked down a moment in quiet reminiscence. "Well, now since you very kindly reminded me how long I've been in the cooler, how about you tell me a song you really like, and I'll have to go and buy that record when I get out."

Banks did not have to think too long for this one. Several things sprung to mind, but there was one song that stood out, and she knew immediately that it was the one.

"I know it," she said, and she let Tom wait for a second, just to see him patiently wait, eyebrows slightly raised and eyes fixed upon her. "It's a Beatles song."

"Yeah, you said them earlier," Tom said, remembering. "They're called the 'beetles?' Like beetle bugs?"

Banks laughed. "Sort of," she said. "But they spell it B-E-A-T-L-E-S. They're from Britain, but they're *extremely* popular here, too. You should see how these kids *scream* when they go on; it's enough to bring the house down! The song I'm thinking of is from a record they put out last year, by the name of, 'Beatles for Sale,' and it's called, 'I'll Follow the Sun.'"

"'I'll Follow the Sun,'" Tom repeated with a serene smile. "I'll remember it. It'll be a couple of decades-old by then, but if they're as good as you say they are, I'm sure they'll be around somewhere."

"I sure hope so." Banks took a moment before pressing Tom to continue his story, all the while hearing the lighthearted and gentle strumming of a guitar-playing somewhere in her mind.

~ 5 ~

EYE TO EYE

* * *

Alright, I guess I'll pick the story up where I left off, hmm? Now, if I remember correctly, I left it havin' just made acquaintance with Miss Diamond, and Miss Betty'd let me know how she liked how I's treatin' her.

Well, that was the start of it, really. Every so often, I'd see one of them little'n's playin' and keepin' her out, or pushin' her over, or makin' fun of her havin' one arm, and all kinds of nonsense like that. They weren't bad kids, though, let me be clear. They just was in their own little world. And Miss Betty and Mrs. McMullen didn't always have the time to keep after all of 'em, 'specially in the summertime like it was. They was just tryna find things to do around there, and they saw Miss Diamond as their new little plaything.

Every time somethin' like that would happen, I'd do my best to stop it and get them little'n's to leave her alone. Of course, I woulda been doin' all that anyhow, but I was keepin' a closer eye because I wanted Miss Betty to see what a nice guy I am, I'll admit it. The one thing I didn't know was Miss Diamond already knew exactly what I was doin'.

One day I'd just got done shooin' little Billy away from her (he'd been grabbin' her empty sleeve and pullin' on it. I don't think he was doin' it to be mean, he was just foolin'), and I went to go back

38

workin' with the animals they had out there in the barn, and she was followin' me.

She said to me as we were walkin' into the barn, "Why do you keep trying to protect me?"

Now, I didn't know what to say to her, but I just told her, "I'm just tryna make sure they know they can't be pickin' on ya, that's all."

I turned around to her, and she was lookin' back at me with this look on her face.

"You want Betty to know you're doin' it," she said.

She always said things like that. She wasn't askin'; she already knew that was what was goin' on.

"You don't like that?" I asked her.

She just shrugged. "Do you love Betty?" She asked me.

Now I don't usually find myself without somethin' to say, as you can imagine, but that was twice now this girl had left me with nothin'.

"I don't know," I said. "I sure do like her, though. Are you alright with that?"

"I don't care," she said. "But why do you want her to see you protectin' me?"

"Well," I said, "because you know she cares whether you're okay or not. She's a nice lady, Miss Betty. She just wants to make sure you're alright, too, and it makes her happy to see me helpin' out."

I had never had a whole conversation with anyone about Betty or anything like it. The only people I ever talked to about anything was the other boys, but even them I wouldn't talk to about somethin' like this.

"That's nice," she decided to say after a bit.

"I thought so," I said.

She was a girl of few words, Miss Diamond. But she never had trouble letting you know what she was thinkin'. She's not like a lot of people that's out there, you know. People will take twenty minutes to tell you something they coulda told ya in two, just because they want to seem like they's smart. You don't have to talk all the time to be smart. Miss Diamond was one of the smartest people I've ever known, and she hardly said a word.

Then, I said to her, "I thought you was gonna be takin' care of yourself?"

She got this annoyed little look on her face. "I tried. Dolly threw a notebook at me yesterday, so I threw it back at her. She told her mamma that I did it, now her mamma said I can't throw things anymore. She never sees the others do it, but when I do it, she yells."

I was feelin' real sorry for Miss Diamond. I knew this kinda thing was gonna happen when they brought her home, and Miss Betty'd known it too. It's not easy to be the outsider, 'specially against people who didn't know what that was like.

"Well," I said. "Maybe you should tell Mrs. that they hit you first."

"It ain't no use," she said. "Adults don't listen, and they don't care."

I remember thinkin' about how she must have come from somethin' awful to think somethin' like that.

I said, "Some of 'em don't, sure. But you know Mrs. went and got you from the home because she wanted to have you here."

She thought about that for a second, and then she said, "I guess."

"And," I said, "if you think adults don't care, then what d'ya call me?"

She looked me up and down and said, "You're a kid, too."

Then I said, "I'll have you know I'll be turnin' eighteen years old soon."

That's when she smiled just a little for the first time since she'd been there, and she said, "A big kid."

That was the end of that conversation. Miss Diamond went off her own way, and I didn't see her for the rest of the day. After I'd got done dealin' with the animals at about two in the afternoon, I was fixin' the barn door. One of the hinges had got all bent up, you know. So I was up on the ladder, tryin' to get new hinges on this old door. That's when Mrs. McMullen came walkin' up to the barn from the house with a cup of water.

When I saw she was comin' over, I got down from the ladder 'cause I didn't wanna be disrespectful if she was comin' to talk to me. Turns out she was.

When she got over to me, she handed me the cup of water and smiled.

"Well, gosh, Mrs. M," I said, taking the water she was offerin' me, "You didn't have to go doin' that, now. But I sure do appreciate it."

And I sure did. Laborin' out there in the Alabama sun was enough to knock a horse over. At least they was in the shade.

I took a drink of the water, and the Mrs. started talkin' to me.

"I saw you were out here with Diamond earlier," she said. "Betty said she was talkin' to you the other day, too."

"Oh, sure," I said, "Miss Diamond's got her own little personality, don't she? She's a good kid, too."

"I think so, too," she said. She was readin' me with her eyes, too. "She told me earlier that the other kids have been pickin' on her."

I said, "Yeah, they're just bein' kids, I guess. They ain't used to her, yet."

"I just don't know why she wouldn't've told me before," Mrs. said.

"Well," I said, "she ain't used to you yet, either."

Mrs. smiled at me again. She'd always had such a pretty smile. That kind of smile only a mother could have, one that makes you feel like everything's alright.

"When I asked her if she was alright after them pickin' on her," she said, "she told me you were lookin' out for her."

"Well, I try," I said. "Just whenever I notice somethin', I try to be helpful."

"I'm sure you do," she said. "Well, I thank you. To be honest with you," she lent in so close when she said this, I could smell her perfume, "it's nice to know someone else cares so much about that child. My husband wasn't too keen on adopting, you know. Especially not," and she dropped all the way down to a whisper, "what he calls, a 'broken child.'"

She stopped leanin' in and looked at me. I wasn't sure what to say. I knew she didn't have a whole lot of people to talk to, but I was pretty sure this wasn't the kind of thing a farmhand oughta know.

"Goodness," I said. "Well, Mrs. M, you can be sure I care, all right. I'll be keepin' an eye out, don't you worry."

I finished my water, and she took the cup back and went on back in the house. I went back to my workin', thinkin' about what the hell it was that just happened. But I was also thinkin' about how anyone could think that child was lesser just because of her not havin' an arm. I guess that's when it really hit me that I cared about her, and I'd be lookin' out, all right. Not just for Mrs. McMullen or for Miss Betty, neither. I'd be lookin' out 'cause I cared enough to do it.

Speakin' of Miss Betty, this is where the story takes a little bit of a turn. It was maybe a few days later now, and Miss Diamond had been followin' me around some while I was workin', just walkin' around, sittin' on the ground near wherever I was. She never said much still, but every so often I'd say somethin', and she'd say somethin' back, and little by little we had a nice little friendship goin'.

We was out in the rows, and I was goin' down the line of trees checkin' for bugs and weeds, just routine. As I walked down, she followed right behind me. I didn't turn around to look at her, but I could hear her tiny footsteps.

I said to her, "You ain't hidin' from them other kids, now, are ya?"

She said, "So what if I am? They don't want to play with me, anyway. And I'm just fine out here."

"Alright," I said, while I was reachin' down pullin' up a weed, "As long as Mrs. M. don't mind you're out here with me."

She said, "She's fine. And Betty thinks I'm better off out here with you, anyway. She said she knows you'll look after me."

It was nice to hear that Miss Betty trusted me with the child. Not that it was surprising. It was just, well, it was just nice.

"Alright, then," I said. Miss Diamond couldn't see my face while I was facin' the other day, but I was smilin', too.

Then, as if she knew we was talkin' about her, Miss Betty came up the rows behind us. We heard her footsteps, so we turned around and saw her comin'. The two of us stopped and waited for her to catch up.

"Diamond," she said, "Mamma says come on in, supper's gonna be ready in a minute."

I looked up at the sky, it was still light, but the sunset was startin'. It was gonna be time for me to leave soon. Miss Diamond looked up at me, then she went along running to the house, leavin' Betty and me alone.

"I do apologize, Miss Betty," I said. "I didn't realize it was that late already."

"It ain't nothin'," she said. "She likes hangin' out with you, and it's one less child for me to look after. I just hope she's not botherin' you."

"Oh, naw," I said, "she ain't botherin' nobody. I'm gettin' my work done just as well, and I guess she's not comfortable enough with the other kids yet. She's sure taken a shinin' to me, though. Can't imagine why."

Miss Betty smiled at me and moved in a bit closer. "You're a good one, Tom Higgins. I always knew it."

Maybe I shouldn't have done it, but I moved in a little myself.

"I sure do try, Miss Betty," I said. "I sure do try."

We got even closer, then we was touchin'. About then, I'd like to say I didn't give in and let myself try somethin', but if I said that, I'd be a liar. We was kissin' now, and I remember feelin' like I was on top of the world. It wasn't just me who went in for it, of course, but when she pulled away, I sure felt guilty. I'd forgot myself, and I was worried she thought I was doin' too much.

"We shouldn't," she said. We was still real close, and she was lookin' up at me with them pretty, bright eyes.

I said, "No, probably not."

She nodded, then we separated a little. She looked so struck, poor thing. She was like a deer in headlights. She started to say somethin, but I stopped her.

"You don't have to go worryin' about it, Miss Betty," I said. "I know how things work. I shouldn't have done that."

"Tom, it wasn't just you," she said. "But I don't know if we can do that again."

"Not another word, Miss Betty," I said. "Put it out of your mind. We can just keep bein' friendly, and I won't bring it up again, I promise."

You gotta understand; I thought I was doin' the right thing. Ladies like Miss Betty didn't end up with farmhands like me. She'd have been better off with a fella who was gonna make her happy, who could give her things and provide. As much as I cared about Miss Betty and still do, I thought it was best to leave it there before things got too painful. I thought that's what she wanted, too.

I should have seen what was goin' on behind those eyes. She stood there lookin' at me, and all I could do was push her away.

"You should probably go in for supper, now," I said. "I'll see you tomorrow."

She nodded and went on back down the row toward the house. The sun was settin', bit by bit, and I knew it was time for me to head out. I got my work gloves and hit the road, knowin' I had done the right thing but feelin' like I'd been run over.

And if that wasn't bad enough, some of the other boys were hangin' around at Johnnie Pritchett's house that night, and I figured it might lift my spirits to hang around with 'em, drinkin' some cheap whiskey somebody'd stolen. Johnnie was the only one out of all the boys who lived with family. He was there with his sister and her husband. Most of the other boys either lodged in some rooms in town or didn't have nowhere at all, so's they just moved around different places all the time. Some of 'em been caught sleepin' in the barn some nights.

No, old Mr. McMullen didn't pay any of us a whole lot to work, but for a lot of us, there wasn't many other places that would take us in. 'Specially for the colored boys. Now, you know they worked the same long days us white boys did, but he'd pay them even less than us, and we already wasn't makin' very much. He was about the only one in Dothan who wanted to pay 'em, though, it's a shame. Ain't no difference, you know? They's workin' the same as me, never understood why they was treated that way.

I was alright for a little while. We was all havin' a good ol' time, lettin' the day go and lettin' the whiskey into our heads. Now, you remember the two from the fight, Jimmy and Tuck? Yeah, they was there, too. Sat as far away from each other as possible in Johnnie's little barn, too (We had to be out in the barn where they kept their couple horses, so's not to disturb Johnnie's sister. She let him live there since his Mamma and Daddy kicked him out, but she wasn't gonna be no accessory to any nonsense, which is exactly the reason we were there, all nineteen or twenty of us).

Yeah, so Jimmy was over by me, and he was talkin' about this big ol' bug he'd seen out in the trees and was askin' me if I'd seen anything like it around. That's when I heard Tuck on the other side, runnin' his mouth to Johnnie and Danny Kitch about things that didn't concern him.

He was sayin', "She's a weird one, too. Now, why them McMullens decided to bring in that crippled kid, I'll never understand. They ain't got enough to pay us any more than pieces, but they got enough to feed another mouth every day. And she's always hangin' around out in the field, where she got no business bein'. I tell ya, they should just take her back where they found her."

"Hold on there, Tuck," I said. Everybody'd been havin' their own conversations, but most of 'em stopped when they heard me call over to him. "Now, you got a point about the money, and I hear ya, but it ain't the kid's fault they brought her in. She got just as much right to be there as anybody."

"You'd say that Tom," he said, and everybody was listenin' now. "You're the one she's been hangin' around. Them McMullen girls just can't stay away from ya, can they?"

There was a snicker here and there, it wasn't like none of the boys knew about my connection with Miss Betty, but they didn't know what had happened that day and how much it hurt.

"Watch it now," I said. "She's just took a shinin' to me, that's all. She's just lookin' for a friend."

"Uh-huh," he said, with a stupid ol' grin on his face, "Miss Betty found a friend in ya, too, did she?"

"Leave him alone, Tuck," Jimmy said, "Tom ain't done nothin' to nobody. Why you gotta start shit all the time?"

That's when Tuck told Jimmy to shut up, callin' him a word I don't like to use. Jimmy was a colored boy, you know, and I think that's why Tuck didn't like him so much. Unlike me, he still kept to that way of thinkin'. He'd never be loud about it, but he was always different with them than he was with the white boys.

Well, when he went and said that, Jimmy got up to get 'im, but I held him back from doin' it. Tuck was standing up now, too. He was already ready to fight. Little Ricky Thomas (he was only fourteen, but he was quick on his feet and just as strong as any one of us, God bless 'im) and Jack Gordon had jumped up to stand in front of Jimmy while I was holdin' him back. They was all yellin' and carryin' on.

"Cool down, now!" I said to 'em, and most of 'em stopped when I said it. "Y'all're better than this, y'hear? We all been workin' out in the sun and got our brains fried, that's all. Ain't nobody gotta start anythin', now."

Nobody moved for a second, they just stayed lookin' between Jimmy and Tuck, and some was lookin' at me, too.

That's when Tuck got disappointed that there wasn't gonna be any fight, I guess. He was always achin' for a breakin'. And bein' the way he was, he decided to make a god awful comment about (and excuse me now, this is just what the sumbitch said) what Miss Diamond was doin' with the one hand she had when she was out there with me. Real bad taste, I know, just awful.

That's when I jumped around in front of them boys and took a lunge at the bastard myself. The boys didn't have time to hold me back before I had him down in the hay. I gave him what I had, and after a few good punches, the other boys lifted me up off of 'im, and Johnnie was yellin' to get everyone calm. He didn't want the cops to be called out there or nothin' (not to mention the horses was startin' to get a little riled up) because he knew they wouldn't be disappointed for an opportunity to give us hell. Oh, excuse me, Detective. I'm sure you wouldn't do a thing like that, but in these parts at that time of night, well, let's just say I'm speakin' from experience.

When all was a little more settled, and everybody'd gotten their minds back with 'em, Jimmy and Jack had me by the shoulders while Tuck was holdin' the side of his face, which was bruisin' up just as the one from the other fight was almost healed. My knuckles was cut up, too, but I had other things I was thinkin' about.

"You ain't nothin' but trouble, Tuck," I said, tryna stay calm after realizing how angry I'd got. "I don't know why you go messin' like you do, but it stops here. You start somethin' like this again, and I'll get you thrown out, you son of a bitch. I can promise you that."

The other boys were backing me up, making comments and all. Tuck looked at me with this real mean look in his eyes, one of which was bloodshot and gettin' purple.

"I'm just sick of you, Tommy," he said. "You got the McMullens all over you. I bet you's gettin' paid more than us, too."

"You know that ain't true, Tuck," I said, "I get paid same way everyone else does. I ain't never said I was any better than anybody. Sure, they like me, but you gotta remember: I've been here longer than most of ya, and my daddy was here 'fore I was. Don't mean nothin'."

Nobody moved. We was all waitin' for Tuck to speak, but I guess he finally ran out of things to say.

After a while, Johnnie said, "Tuck, why don't you go out and get some air or somethin'?"

Now, we all knew that really meant Johnnie was tellin' him he should leave, and no one was objectin'. So he looked at me one more time and went ahead and left. Jimmy and Jack let go of my shoulders, and I just looked down, not wantin' to catch anyone's eye.

When Tuck was gone, Johnnie came up to me and said, "You'd better keep an eye around your place tonight, Tommy. We've all had somethin' tonight, and sometimes boys get a little too riled up and wanna go mess with somethin'."

"I know, Johnnie, thank you," I said.

* * *

~ 6 ~

IN HIS OWN WORDS

Tom had answered Banks' original question, but she still had a million more.

She now knew how the boys from before figured into the story, most significantly, one Alan Tucker Holt, known to everyone that knew him as "Tuck." The tension that arose between Tuck and Higgins was clear and unsurprising.

There was also the matter of Tom's budding, then faltering, relationship with Betty McMullen. As off-topic as this portion of Tom's story seemed at first, Banks began to think there was more to be had from that story than she initially thought.

In addition, and perhaps most interestingly, there was the new friendship between Tom and Diamond McMullen. Even though he insisted that she was not involved in the end, he was keen on developing the story between them. Now Banks knew that she had served as a point of contention between Higgins and Tuck, but was it possible she was in the story solely for that purpose?

The answer, Banks decided, was perhaps. Not only was the young Diamond at the source of the conflict between them, but she also served as a connection detail leading not only to Betty but also to her mother, Violet McMullen. Now that Banks had learned more about the setting of the stage, and the relationships between people around that orchard, one common element in all sides of the story was Miss Diamond McMullen. And to make it even more interesting, the one testimonial that could turn this entire case on its head was from a person who had gone missing the night of the crime and had never been found. Could that *really* be a coincidence?

Banks pondered all of this while she sat across from Higgins as he recounted days gone by. He told most of the story while looking down at the table in front of him, intensely concentrating on the details, probably hoping nothing had escaped him. Or, perhaps, that he had missed just the right amount of information from the story.

When Tom had finished speaking, he looked up at Banks, who was looking down at the notes she had collected. There was undoubtedly no wondering why her hand was beginning to cramp. You would think she had written down every word he'd said for the past hour and a half.

"Got all ya need?" He asked her, teasing.

She looked up at him as he grinned at her.

"Well, I'm starting to understand why everyone's so interested in Miss Diamond McMullen," she said. "That's for sure."

"Yeah," said Higgins, "They'd only just started to realize how close she was to everything when they did me in. The Dothan fuzz been askin' about if she was involved last time they were questionin' me. The truth is," he looked to make sure she was paying attention, "we was all messed up in one way or another, anyway. She was just that one thing that sent the dominos fallin' down. But she didn't mean to do it; she was just in the wrong place at the wrong time."

Banks made a mental note to remember that last part. Usually, you would make a comment like that about someone when something had happened to them. Maybe something had, and maybe Tom Higgins knew all about it.

"I'm sure she didn't mean to cause trouble," Banks said.

"Oh, I didn't say that," Tom said, laughing. "She sure caused plenty of trouble all right and meant every bit of it. But I can tell you more about that next time."

As if on cue, the guard tapped on the glass pane bolted in the middle of the steel door, signaling that Banks' time had run out. Banks involuntarily slumped, just a little, wishing for whatever reason that she could stay and listen for longer.

"Next time," she said. "Thank you, Tom."

"Always a pleasure, Detective."

02:16 PM.

Banks sat at her desk in the bullpen of the station later that same day, the Beatles still playing in her mind. She felt content thinking of the playful conversation she and Tom Higgins had had earlier, but she shook it from her mind. She knew that she had limited time to make anything of this case, and she was working fervently to put all the pieces together.

The bullpen of the police station was a reasonably large yet somehow crowded room, with plain linoleum floors and fluorescent lights. The paint on the walls was a pale blue, but all of the scuffs and aging made it look a little empty of color. The desks were uniform to each other, stuffed in rows, and cornered to fit as many as possible. Against the walls, there were filing cabinets and tables stacked with folders and piles of paper. There were two hallways on the left side leading to evidence and archives and interrogation and holding. Against the walls were photographs of the Sergeant and Captain, photographs of Montgomery, and various plaques and declarations of the police force's successes over the years.

At the farthest end of the bullpen were doors to the offices of Sgt. Nichols and Captain Roy Johnston, the latter office of which many new detectives, including Banks, had never seen. The Captain had been dealing with fairly severe health conditions as of late. Therefore, and until notice, the station was primarily run by the

Sergeant. The Captain only intervened within the station for serious matters.

There were other officers around, sitting at their desks, eating lunch, and chatting. Some were working on their own cases with a lighthearted groove, while Banks worked with competitive diligence.

Now that she had fresh information to add to the puzzle, she figured now would be a good time to review what had already been there. Perhaps there was a connection she missed between Higgins' story and the proceedings in the courtroom or a piece of evidence.

Banks laid the files out as much as she could and began reading. At the very top of the pile was the court report itself, and she read the beginning of it for the thousandth time, just for the sake of routine:

Thomas HIGGINS v. STATE of Alabama.

Supreme Court of Alabama.

September 26, 1955.

CAULFIELD, Justice.

Conrad MATTHEWS, Esq.

David BOYD, Esq. Defending.

Thomas Higgins was tried and found guilty in Houston County under an indictment for two counts of murder in the second degree. This indictment charged that Higgins killed both his employer, Roger McMullen, and Alan Tucker Holt, whom he worked with at the McMullen Farm and Orchard. Higgins was charged with killing the two men with a revolver pistol after engaging in adultery for some time with Roger Mc-Mullen's wife.

Banks shivered a little at the last detail. She had already known about the affair, of course, but it felt a little more real now. After hearing Tom mention the friendly nature of his and Mrs. Mc-Mullen's relationship, knowing where it would eventually lead made the buildup somewhat awkward and creepy to read. It was certainly one of the more random details in the cornucopia of issues that once lived at the McMullen residence.

There was some secondhand relief, too, after rereading this portion. Because Tom Higgins was charged with secondary murder, he had already been less likely to be put to death. This was, of course, because Tom's acts had decidedly been spur-of-the-moment, meaning that neither shot had been planned. However, there had been some debate at the time about whether one or both of the shots *had* been intended. This was mainly due to the question of why Tom had his gun at the time.

The court report continued with the attorneys' details, a few different witnesses called, terms of the charges, etc. Banks was most looking forward to getting to the transcript of Tom Higgins on the witness stand, where he was questioned by Mr. Conrad Matthews, the attorney against him. When she finally got to that point, she found that it read just slightly differently than when she had skimmed it before. It was one thing for Tom Higgins to be a faceless killer, but putting his face and his mannerisms into the reading was another story entirely.

Q: Mr. Higgins, you were an employee of Roger McMullen's down there on the orchard. Is that correct?

A: Yes, sir.

Q: And what kind of work did he have you doing there?

A: Oh, odds and ends, you know. Farm labor, repairing, taking care of the trees, landscaping, all kinds of things.

Q: And he paid you well for it?

A: Well, he paid me. I don't know about *well*, but I never complained. I'm still not.

Q: Did you ever wish to be paid more?

A: If I'm honest, sir, it never crossed my mind. All the boys were paid about the same. Whatever they were getting is what I took.

Q: Alright, then. Did you ever have any disagreements with Mr. McMullen before the night in question?

A: No, sir, not one. I don't think he cared to speak to any of the boys that often. I rarely talked to him.

Q: Interesting. Switching gears a little bit, tell me this. How long were you engaging in sexual relations with his wife, Mrs. Violet McMullen?

A: Just a couple of weeks, sir.

Q: Now, if you'll tell me, who was the instigator to the beginning of this little relationship?

A: I'd say it was mutual, sir.

Q: Would she say the same, Mr. Higgins, if we asked her?

A: I'd say so, sir. Although if you're asking me if I enjoyed myself, I won't deny it.

Banks could almost hear the muffled laughter in the courtroom. She could see him, sitting there, eighteen years old, playing for the enjoyment of others as it seemed was his specialty, hoping to God it would get him something. If only she had been in the room to see it. Instead, she pushed up her cat-eye glasses and kept reading.

Q: That's quite enough of that. Let's bring it to the night of the twenty-first, Mr. Higgins. You and Violet McMullen were in the upstairs bedroom engaging in sexual intercourse while her husband, Roger, was away for the night. Is that correct?

A: Well, we weren't exactly all the way into it, sir. We were just kissing that time.

Q: But would you say that it would eventually lead to intercourse, had it been allowed to continue?

A: Yes, sir. I would say it was likely.

Q: It's good that you didn't bother to deny it because pieces of your clothing remained in the bedroom after you had left it, clothing that you have already identified in addition to a rucksack. So then, at around ten o'clock, Mr. McMullen returned to the house. Can you take me through what happened after that?

A: Yes, sir. Well, Mr. McMullen wasn't very happy, as you can imagine. He came upstairs and found us there. Well, he went on yelling and all, and he told me to get up, and we were going to go outside. So I did as he told me, and he took me out to the barn.

Q: The barn where you shot him?

A: The only barn on the premises, yes, sir.

Q: And when the two of you were in the barn, you began to fight?

A: I would say we were fighting before we reached the barn, but yes, sir, that's what was going on.

Q: And it was just the two of you in there?

A: Us and a couple of cows.

Banks herself let out a snort there. This prompted a couple of other officers to look over at her, and she quickly cleared her throat and pretended it had been a cough or something. Wild, who was sitting at his desk, which formed a right angle with her own, looked up and raised his eyebrows once, then they both continued their respective workings.

Q: Yes, thank you, Mr. Higgins. But there were no other people in the barn when you entered, correct?

A: Yes, sir, that is correct.

Q: So, then, how did Mr. Holt become involved in the scene?

A: Well, I guess he had stayed behind for something; I don't know why he was there. But he had probably seen us go in, or he heard something was going on in the barn, and so he came to see what it was.

Q: And he found the two of you in there?

A: He sure did, sir.

Q: So let me tell you what I think, Mr. Higgins. I think that when Mr. Holt found Mr. McMullen and yourself in there fighting, that Mr. McMullen turned around to see who was behind him, and you took advantage of this moment when you did not have his full attention, took out your pistol, and shot him. And then you shot Mr. Holt, who had been a witness to your crime.

A: That's quite the story you got there.

Q: You mean to tell me you didn't shoot these men? Do keep in mind, Mr. Higgins, that you are under oath. And let's not forget the blood, which matches your blood type, which neither of the victims shared with you, found in proximity to the bodies as well as trailed to where the Dothan officers found you.

A: That is true, sir.

Q: And in addition, Mr. Higgins, you cited the exact model of the .38 revolver that acted as the murder weapon when you were questioned just this week, a weapon that matched the kind of ammunition found in both victims. For the sake of clarity, would you repeat the model for us today?

A: Yes, sir, I did, and that's a Smith and Wesson Victory Model, sir. About ten years old, God bless America.

Q: And I'd like to add that when the police searched your residence, they found a good many other guns, too. What are you doing with all those guns in your house, son?

The report showed that the defense attorney, a Mr. David Boyd, who had been assigned to Tom as a public defender since he could not afford his own lawyer, decided to make his first objection because this was a personal inquiry and unrelated to the case. But the judge overruled the objection and allowed the questioning to continue.

A: Don't worry about it. I don't have any problem telling you. Those guns in the house were my daddy's, sir. He fought in the war and liked to hunt. There's paperwork in the kitchen drawer for every one of them, too.

Q: Coming back to that weapon, may I remind the court that you still have not told anyone its location?

A: I do not know where it is, sir. I threw it away somewhere along the road in the dark. Someone must have picked it up. There are lots of poor boys like me around here, and that's a good pistol. If they don't keep it, they could sell it.

Q: So you hid it when you were running away from the scene.

A: Yes, sir.

Q: You stumbled away from the scene with injuries, leaving all the obvious evidence behind. Did you think you could get away, son?

Banks wasn't sure if it would have been appropriate for another objection at that moment, but she thought it was an unfair question. She also did not know why she was compelled to side with Tom, perhaps because she now had met him, and this attorney who questioned him seemed *mean*, somehow, which was crazy. After all, successfully convicting a murderer was precisely what Banks would have considered a win for the law.

So, why do I feel so conflicted?

A: I didn't know what would happen, sir. I was afraid.

Q: You were afraid? If you were so scared, perhaps you should not have committed this crime in the first place.

A: Yes, sir.

Q: So why did you have the gun on you in the first place, Mr. Higgins? You had gone to the house that night to be with Mrs. McMullen. You didn't, perhaps, plan on shooting her, too?

A: No, sir, I would never. She never did anything wrong to anyone.

Q: And Roger McMullen did? Defending his household from the likes of you, a gutter rat with no respect and no future?

Thereof, the record included the judge telling Mr. Matthews to calm down, but there was no further repercussion for his behavior or threat. Again, Banks found herself backing what should have been the wrong horse. Higgins was a murderer, sure. But was it really necessary to tear him down like that? Banks wondered whether it was only because she had met him that she felt that way, especially since their conversation had been just a little more than the cold procedure it usually would have been.

Q: Can I tell you what I think happened, Mr. Higgins?

A: I'd sure be surprised if you didn't, sir.

Q: I think you went there that night intending to stay until Mr. McMullen arrived home. And you planned to kill him with that pistol you brought with you. Maybe it was your idea, or maybe Violet McMullen asked you to do it, but either way, I don't know why you would have brought a fully loaded weapon with you if you did not plan to use it.

An objection. Matthews suggested that the charge was first-degree murder when the court had already decided that the murders were secondary. There was no evidence to suggest that the theory was valid.

A: I never planned a murder, sir.

Q: Fine. But you did commit one, didn't you? Planned or not, you committed murder that night.

A: With all due respect, he was beating me, sir.

Q: I'm sure he was, but a strong young man like yourself, you could have taken that opportunity to overpower him, not shoot him.

A: Yes, sir.

Q: I'm sure you had reservations about the man you worked for already. You couldn't have had much respect for him; why else would you have an affair with his wife?

A: She was unhappy, sir.

Q: You question a dead man's ability to take care of his wife and family adequately? Your disrespect knows no bounds, Mr. Higgins.

A: Yes, sir.

Q: You're a murderer, aren't you, son?

A: It would seem so, sir.

Q: Last question before the court. Do you regret what you did?

A: I don't, sir. And I never will.

Reviewing this testimony only made Banks feel more in the dark, not because there were no new details, but because she was starting to feel like maybe there *was* no more to this case. It seemed pretty open and shut, as it had been reported to be. It was certainly more interesting to learn about, but Banks shuddered at the thought that that bigot Sergeant was right. However much she cared about the details about this case, and still had more questions, maybe it was just what she had said herself: a passion project.

However, Banks knew well that passion projects are never worthless endeavors. She still had her feeling that there was more to be known, so she decided then that even if that didn't end up changing anything on the surface, she would feel better knowing for sure. Anything would be better than the feeling of anxious un- certainty sitting in her stomach.

As long as I don't lose my job along the way, she thought.

~ 7 ~

WHEN ONE DOOR CLOSES

MONDAY, JULY 26, 1965. 07:59AM.

Banks was beginning to find routine in these visits to the penitentiary in Dothan. Regardless of waking up early to get down there for her time slot, she always found herself with energy, excited to listen and ask questions. She was also thankful that Tom Higgins was not a bad storyteller. She imagined she might feel differently about this situation if the person she was seeing was a snooze to talk to.

After arriving right on time, three days after the last visit, the same guard showed her to the solitary confinement cell, where Tom Higgins was, once again, waiting patiently for her.

"Good mornin', Detective," he said to her when they were alone. He waved one of his cuffed hands at her as he said it. "Been listenin' to any bug songs since I saw ya?"

"Good morning, Tom," she replied, giggling as she settled into the metal chair. "And I often do. You know, I never asked you what your favorite song was last time."

"Oh, my!" Tom said, looking up at the ceiling, straining for an answer.

"See?" Banks teased. "It's not so easy, is it?"

Tom smiled, still looking up. After a moment, he brought his gaze back down, having come up with something to say.

"You know, this is a strange choice," he said. "You might be too young to remember, 'Unchained Melody?'"

"Tom, I am a year older than you!" Banks exclaimed, laughing again as Tom feigned shock.

"I cannot believe it, Detective," he said. "I thought you musta been about twenty. I would say I like older women, but that's probably in bad taste."

"I would agree, Tom." Banks rolled her eyes in complete awe of herself. The two of them talked like friends, and Banks never made a habit of being friendly with criminals before.

"Figured so," Tom said. "Well, then you would know, I guess, that that song was real big in '55, and a buncha guys sang it and put their own spin on it. There's all kinds of versions out there, but my favorite was Al Hibbler. And sure, it's a sappy song, but it's gentle on the heart. I'd love to hear that song again."

"I know it," Banks said, watching Tom fall back into his memories again. She could not help but feel a touch of sadness, sat there in the cement and steel, only able to imagine what it was like to be trapped in there for so many years.

She snapped herself out of this train of thought, reminding herself that Tom still had the potential to be a ruthless killer, however much she had already convinced herself that she didn't want him to be.

"Alright, Tom," she said. "Ready to talk some more?"

"Well," he said, coming down from the clouds, "'round here ain't much need for me to be talkin' to nobody. Ain't nobody wanna listen to me, anyway."

"Well, I'm here for just that reason, Tom."

"And I sure do thank you for it, Detective."

* * *

If my memory serves me, August was just beginnin', and me and Tuck had just had that fight down at Johnnie's. We didn't let each other forget it, neither.

He never came after me or nothin', the other boys made sure of that, all right, but he'd always be lookin' at me whenever I was anywhere near 'im, 'specially when Miss Diamond was with me.

That was almost all the time, too. Miss Diamond was stickin' around with me almost every day. Her mamma didn't care, and I didn't mind the company when the boys were workin' elsewhere. I hardly saw Miss Betty around for a good while there. S'pose she was avoidin' me.

It was nice that Miss Diamond found a friend in me because she didn't really have anyone else. I already told ya how the other kids were with her, and she didn't have any friends from the life she had before, so I guess she clung to me like she did because I was the only one who showed any interest.

Around that time is when she started tellin' me about herself a little. Because I'm sure you can tell, I do like to talk, and I like to ask questions about people. So I asked her one day when I was fixin' a couple of broken boards on the fence on the outside of the property, and she was handin' me nails. I asked her about what her life was like before she came there.

"Why do you wanna know?" She asked me.

"Well," I said while I was hammerin', "we's friends, now, ain't we? Figure I should know a little somethin' about you."

"We're friends?" She asked,

"Well, sure," I said. "You got any of them?"

"No," she said. "I don't have any friends."

"Well, if I'm honest," I said, "I don't really have any friends, neither. Them boys out here are good ol' boys, but I can't say I talk to 'em much about nothin' important."

"We don't talk about nothin' important, either," she said.

I said, "Well, that's because you don't talk about nothin' at all."

We kept movin' down the line on that fence out there. Think some kid went around there kickin' the boards in; there was loose ones all along the damn thing. I kept hammerin', and she kept handin' me nails.

"Well, what do you wanna talk about?" She asked.

"I don't know," I said. "You wanna tell me about the home? Did you ever have any family, or were you always there?"

"Are you writin' a book?" she asked me.

I just laughed. "You don't have to tell me if you don't wanna."

She thought for a second, and then she said, "I wanna make a deal."

I had no idea what she meant, so I just looked at her. "What kinda deal?" I asked.

"I'll tell you about the home," she said, "and you tell me why you and Betty can't be together."

I was a little surprised she wanted to know about that. I wondered what she had heard about what happened with Betty and me, but I'm sure she noticed that we wasn't talkin' to each other anymore.

"Okay," I said. "You go first."

So she went on tellin' me about the home. It was a little worse than what I thought it would be if I'm honest. I knew it wasn't the most savory of places, but I didn't realize just how bad.

She'd gone to live at the home when she was four. Before that, she did have a family, kinda. She was born with only one arm, said her mamma and daddy didn't like her too much because of it. Some people just don't have any sense. Her mamma pitied her, though, so she was alright. But then her mamma died, and her daddy didn't care if she stayed or went, and I guess he didn't see any point keepin' her, so he dropped her off at the home and took off.

She said she only saw an adult there a few times in all the years she was there. The offices those couple people worked in were completely separate from the home itself, so they didn't have to

be in there with the kids if they didn't want to. She said someone would come by to adopt sometimes, and one of 'em would
come in, grab a child, see if the family liked 'em, and then that
kid would either be gone, or they'd come back for another kid.
The parents lookin' to adopt never went in the home. If they did,
they'd've known what it was like in there.

Miss Diamond mostly just used it as a roof to sleep under. From
what it sounded like, the state was givin' money for them to look
after the kids, and they'd keep up the building on the outside
and in the office, so it looked decent, but they didn't spend any
of that money takin' care of them kids. Inside, the home was all
fallin' apart. There was no food, no nothin'. Miss Diamond said
the kids would go around Montgomery beggin' and stealin' anywhere they could, and there were a lot of times she went to sleep
havin' eaten nothin' at all.

All them kids in that home had some kinda problems, she said.
Couple of 'em had physical problems like she did, but most of 'em
had problems in the head. It wasn't always too bad, but she said
some of 'em were plain crazy. I guess you would be if you lived
like that.

The worst of it was they'd get goin' sometimes lookin' for a
fight, and Miss Diamond was an easy target because she was only
a little thing, not to mention missin' an arm. She said she got
good at fightin' 'em off, but they wouldn't think twice about goin'
for her as often as they saw her. So Miss Diamond would find a
corner to go and sleep in most of the time, puttin' stuff around
her, so she was hidden. She spent all her days hidin', fightin', and
starvin'.

"So I guess that's why you wanna take care of yourself," I said
after she finished.

"Yeah," she said. "I always take care of myself."

"Well," I said, "you must be so happy you got a friend to look
after ya, now."

She smiled a little bit. She didn't smile all the time, but when she did, it was like everything was calm. For that little girl to smile, there had to be some real peace goin' on in the world.

"Your turn," she said. "How come you and Betty can't be together?"

"Well," I said, "it's a little bit complicated, Miss Diamond." By now, the fence was done, and we was sittin' on it, just lookin' across the fields and rows.

"We're just too different," I explained. "She's got a whole life, you know. She's got prospects, education, money; she can't be with someone who's the ground beneath her feet. I ain't got any of that. It's a man's job to support his lady, Miss Diamond. And it's too late for me to be the man she needs to be with, so she's better off findin' somebody else who is. And I figured I should stop before it gets too painful."

Now, I don't mean a lady can't do for herself, Detective, please don't misunderstand. The McMullens was traditional folk, is all. They wanted Miss Betty to be taken care of, and I didn't want her to have to work if she didn't want to because I couldn't make enough for both of us.

Now, Miss Diamond was a firecracker, I've said it before. Not to mention she was only young. She didn't have time for any of that.

"But do you love her?" She asked me.

"Miss Diamond, you gotta understand," I said. "Sometimes for things to work, love just ain't enough. All that you seen in the city; you should know that already."

Knowin' just what to say like always, she said, "If my daddy woulda loved me, I wouldn't have been in the home, to begin with."

"I know that," I said, "but then I wouldn't have my friend."

She smiled again.

Couple of days went by, and then it was the sixth. I remember the day because it was one of the worst days of my whole life.

It was nighttime. Miss Diamond had long since gone inside, and the rest of the boys were gone. I remember I was feelin' a little down already because Little Ricky had got real sick. A couple of the other boys were sayin' he could hardly get up. It had happened before that a kid would come down with somethin' so bad it took 'em. Most times, we never found out what it was that did 'em. And I told ya before: Little Ricky was only fourteen. It was hard to hear for a lot of us.

I was feelin' just awful, and I'd been tryin' to work to distract myself, and 'fore I knew it was dark. So I was walkin' up the rows, about to hit the road.

I got all the way up to the house when I heard gigglin' comin' from the barn. I wondered if them little'n's was outside when they shouldn't be, so I went over to see what was goin' on. I wish I hadn't.

The door was just a little open, so I peeked my head in. What I saw, I just couldn't believe. Miss Betty was in there with Tuck, kissin' and carryin' on. He had his hands on her, 'nough to make me sick. I thought about walkin' away, pretendin' I ain't seen nothin'. My pride got the best of me if I'm honest with ya. I went on in there and made myself known.

"What the hell's goin' on in here?" I said, and Miss Betty looked like she was gonna jump out of her skin. Tuck didn't say nothin'; he just looked at me that same way. He didn't even look happy about what he'd just done to me. Almost made it worse.

"Miss Betty, I got half a mind to tell your daddy who you was out here with," I said. "You know he won't like to hear it."

"Half a mind's all you got," Tuck said. I swear I've never wanted to hit somebody more than then. You might not believe me, but I was never a violent man. I never wanted to fight like I did right then.

"Tuck, you better shut the hell up," I said, "'cause when I tell ol' Mr. McMullen you was out here with his daughter, he's gonna tell you to hit the road."

"What about you, Higgins?" He said, and he came over and got in my face. "I could tell him about you, huh? Think he won't tell you the same thing?"

"I know he would," I said. "But you ain't got shit on me, Tuck. Nothin' ever happened with me."

"Yeah?" And started to back up. I was ready for him to do something—anything except what he did.

"Hey, somebody!" He started yellin'. "They's in here!"

Then he ran past me, and I tried to catch him, but he was gone before I knew what was goin' on. I said, "Oh, I'll kill you, you son of a bitch." Then me and Miss Betty just looked at each other, all wide-eyed. Then we ran, too.

Now the barn had a big ol' front door facin' towards the house where Tuck went out. But in the back of the barn, one of the big ol' slats that made the walls up was real loose, and if you pushed it hard enough, you could fit out that way. Not thirty seconds after he yelled, I could see a flashlight comin'. I led Miss Betty to the back and pushed the slat so we could get out. We went around to the side wall, seein' the flashlight shinin' in between the boards. We snuck around, careful not to make too much noise. I put my head around the corner just in time to see Mr. McMullen come back out of the barn with his flashlight and start back toward the house. Mrs. McMullen was standing up on the back porch, watching him. He looked up at her when he got close and put his hands up like he didn't know what happened out there. The two of them went back in the house, and I realized I'd been holding my breath, and I let it go.

I looked back at Miss Betty, who was clinging to the wall behind me, and from what I could see of her face from the lights on the house, she looked like she could just melt right there.

"It's alright, Miss Betty," I said. "I'm not gonna tell your daddy."

She sighed a little, but she still looked worried.

She said, "Tom, I'm sorry you saw what you saw."

I got off the wall and started walking away into the dark. Miss Betty started followin' behind me. The reason I walked away is 'cause I didn't want her to see me upset, but she had somethin' she wanted to say, so I turned around to look at her. I could barely see her face, but there was just a little bit of light hittin' the tears on her cheeks.

"Miss Betty, you don't have to worry about that," I said. "I'll let it be."

She said, "I wish you wouldn't. Tom, I didn't want you to see that, but it hurts to see you so indifferent now that you did."

"Well, what do you want me to say?" I asked her, trying not to be too loud in case her daddy came back out. "You want me to be angry, huh? You want me to tell you that I don't like you kissin' another guy? Is that what you want? Because I'll stand here and say it because it's true. But how is me gettin' angry about this makin' anything any better? It don't matter how I feel about it, does it?"

She said, "It matters to me. I just wanna know that you care."

I said, "You already know that I care. That's why this has gone on for long enough. This can't go anywhere, Betty. You said it yourself: we can't do this. What I don't understand is why we can't do that, but you and Tuck can go around doin' whatever. How far was y'all gonna go if I hadn't caught ya?"

"How dare you, Tom Higgins!" she yelled at me, then I was shushin' her. "You know I ain't fast like that! He ain't nothin' to me, either. I was sad and confused, and I just wanted to feel somethin'."

"Well, go on!" I said. "But if I can say somethin', you can do a whole lot better than Tuck Holt."

She was cryin' more now, poor thing. I didn't wanna be makin' her cry, but I'd held it in for long enough.

"It ain't about who he is," she said. "And it ain't about who you are, either. I don't care who I'm supposed to be with; I'm tired of carin'. I really like you, Tom Higgins, I don't care what that means, and I don't care what anyone says."

I was back and forth, wantin' to give it a chance, but already hurtin' and not wantin' to be anymore. I knew what would happen. It wasn't just the expectation. Her daddy held my livelihood in the palm of his hand, and if he didn't want me around his daughter, he'd send me walkin'. I had nowhere else to go. I planted my feet and stuck to what I thought was the right thing, and it took everything I had.

"I know you don't care, Miss Betty," I said. "But I can't let you keep doin' this to me or yourself. I can't do this back and forth with you no more. You're the one who said we shouldn't, and you were right."

She said, "I wish you would've fought for me, Tom."

So I said, "I wish you wouldn't have given me a fight."

That's when I left her there. You know, I always wonder if it ever coulda been different, but then I think that if I keep thinkin' that, it's just gonna be all that more painful. Everything I did, I did for a reason. Everything.

* * *

08:49AM.

Banks couldn't help but take a moment in her analysis of his story to feel the undeniable sadness of young heartbreak. She also couldn't help but notice the difference between the way Tom spoke about Betty now, in comparison to how he talked about her in the tape from ten years ago. He had only said that she might have liked him back then, but he never said anything about this.

I suppose he didn't want to be honest about their connection, she thought, *in case it made him look even worse in court. The attorney al-*

ready made him look like a predator upon the McMullen family. What would he have said about this?

She also considered that maybe the difference lay in the time that had passed. Perhaps it was easier at the time, with everything else at the focal point of Tom's attention, to shrug off the short, though meaningful relationship between the two of them. Now that time had passed, however, and Tom had been given all the time in the world to sit and reflect upon his free life, he could feel the severity of the emotional blow he experienced that day. Hindsight, as they say, is twenty-twenty, but it's easier to believe you were right than submitting to 'what if' for years. Whether or not Tom's decision was a mistake could be debated, but it was clear that he felt that moment as clearly now as when he had experienced it a decade ago.

Aside from the heartbreak, Banks thought now about the ever-elevating tension between Tom and Tuck. Notably, Tom even said that he threatened to kill him, which stuck out as a critical point in the dialogue, considering he eventually made good on his promise.

The thing that was still bothering Banks was this: there was a clear and prolonged motive, however maladjusted, for Tom to kill Tuck, but according to the attorney, Tuck had not been the primary victim. Where the bodies had been, concerning where Tom's blood was, even suggested that this was the scenario that made the most sense. Tom had never explicitly agreed in the transcript that the attorney's scenario was entirely accurate to what happened, which blurred the picture for Banks now. Was it possible that Tuck was the actual target and Mr. McMullen complicated the picture? Were the two of them in cahoots, where Tuck tipped off Mr. McMullen to the affair to get under Tom's skin?

Or perhaps Tuck *was* just a witness, and Tom, having already killed someone, indulged in a selfish fantasy and killed a person he hated because what more did he have to lose?

There were so many questions and not nearly enough answers. The good thing was that Banks had been notified that there was deep cleaning happening in the cell blocks that day, and no one would notice if Tom were not in attendance, so she could get away with a little more time. Knowing there was still time, she asked some questions before allowing Higgins to continue.

"Is that why you killed Tuck, then?" she asked.

He came out of his glassy storytelling state and looked her in the eyes. The flash of pure youth that glimmered there surprised her, and then it was gone.

"Well," he said, laughing a little, "not exactly. Though I'd be lyin' if I said it didn't cross my mind."

"You *did* threaten to do it, didn't you?" she pressed him, but only lightly. There was the beginning of trust in their rapport, and she didn't want to jeopardize it by being too official.

"I did," he sighed. "I never planned on makin' good on it, though. Kids just say shit like that, you know. I know it doesn't look good, but seein' as I'm already in here, I'm thinkin' lyin' won't do me much good."

"I suppose so," Banks replied.

~ 8 ~

YOU SCRATCH MY BACK

* * *

It's funny you ask about what I was plannin' on doin' about the Tuck situation because I was havin' the same conversation with Diamond the next day. Little rascal said she looked out her window and saw me goin' in the barn the night before, then saw Tuck runnin' out. She was gonna go down there, but that's when Mr. McMullen went out there, and she knew she'd find out sooner or later. So she asked me about it, and I told her.

"You should beat him up," she said.

I just laughed at her. "Yeah, I thought about that," I said. "But I don't think I'm goin' to."

"Why not?" she asked me.

"He ain't worth it, Miss Diamond," I said. "He's just a bully. Plus, all I gotta do is spread word around, and someone else'll take care of it for me."

"When I would have bullies," she said, "the best way to get them to leave me alone was to beat 'em up."

"I know," I said. "But I'm gettin' to be an adult soon, Miss Diamond. Sometimes you gotta be the bigger man and let it go. Plus,

I'm done playin' this game with him. He'll get what's comin' to 'im eventually."

She let that conversation go, but she still wasn't satisfied with the answer I gave her. I didn't know that she was gonna take the matter into her own hands, or just the one hand, I guess.

Not too long after that, all us boys were walkin' up the road to the farm. It was early; the sun was still comin' up. We'd go down the road, and more would tag along until there was a line of us goin' up the road together like we did every mornin'.

I was walkin' behind Johnnie and in front of Jimmy. Every so often, we'd say somethin' to each other when we was walkin', but a lot of times, we was too tired. This mornin' was different, though, because Tuck looked back at me from about five ahead with that same mean look, and his face was all cut up and bruised again. As you can imagine, this wasn't an unusual look for him. He was always ready to fight, but he was never very good at blockin' his face. I wasn't all that surprised about what he looked like that mornin', even though it was a good deal more than usual.

No, what caught *my* attention was that when he turned back around, I heard Johnnie snort in front of me, then he turned his head to the side and said to me, "he don't look too good this mornin', do he?"

"Naw," I said, "what happened to him this time?"

"I thought you knew already," he said. "He got took to the barn last night by a couple boys and, uh, somebody else, too."

"What'd'ya mean?" I asked him.

Then Jimmy chipped in from behind me and said, "your little friend had us take him in there and hold him down so she could get a hittin' on 'im."

"*Miss Diamond* did that to him?" I asked them. They was just gigglin', and I heard a couple other boys around 'em gigglin', too.

"Sure did," Johnnie said. "She ain't miss 'im once, neither."

Jimmy said, "It was a pleasure to help her out, Tommy. You know I didn't mind keepin' 'im down."

"C'mon, boys," I said. I was smilin' with 'em, but I was tryin' to pretend I was upset. "You know that ain't in good taste. You gotta give 'im a chance to defend himself."

"You mean we shoulda let him at her?" Johnnie asked, still laughin'. "Now, *that* ain't in good taste. And not like we could say no, right? After all, she is our boss a little bit, ain't she?"

"She sure is," I said.

"And you know," Jimmy said, "I'm thinkin' he won't be botherin' you much no more, now that everybody knows a little girl beat 'im up."

"Yeah," I said. "That'll be nice, I guess. Y'all know I ain't put her up to that, right?"

"You didn't have to," Johnnie said. "She was angry as can be. That little girl's a friend of yours, Tommy."

"Yeah," I said. "That's for sure."

So, as you can imagine, I was a little disappointed that she'd done that, but I couldn't stop smilin' all the way to the house. By the time we got there, the sun was almost all the way up. Miss Diamond was sittin' on the back porch when we came around the house. She was waitin' for me to get there. I saw her give Tuck a dirty look when he walked past.

Everybody scattered 'cept for me, Johnnie and Jimmy, and Kitch, too, who I guess was also involved. They stayed there for a second with me when I went up to Miss Diamond, who got down off the porch and come to meet me, lookin' a little nervous, like she was thinkin' I was gonna yell at her. Again, I told you before, kids don't do that because they regret what they did; they do it because they don't wanna get yelled at. I wasn't gonna yell at her, but I figured I'd play it up a little.

So I put my hands on my hips, real straight-faced, and I said, "I heard about what happened last night."

She just kept lookin' up at me. "Are you mad?" she said.

"Well, you know, I told ya I didn't wanna do all that," I said.

She looked down at the ground. I looked around at the other boys behind me, and they were thinkin' I was mad, too. But then I looked back at Miss Diamond, and while I was turnin' around, I caught sight of Miss Betty in the kitchen window. I looked up at her while she was lookin' at me and let myself feel a little bit of pride.

"Guess it's a good thing I didn't have to," I said.

I heard them boys start laughin' behind me, and Miss Diamond looked up to see me smilin', and she started smilin', too. She even started laughin' a little along with the other boys. I went and gave her a little push on the shoulder and said, "Well, come on, then." And we all went out into the barn to get our tools and such and went on workin'. Miss Diamond stayed along with me like she always did.

It was a nice little friendship we had goin' on. She was startin' to really trust me, and I was really enjoyin' havin' her around. We didn't talk too much, just enjoyed each other's company while I was workin'. I never let her do any of the workin' 'cept for one time.

It was gettin' to the end of August, and there was just one or two apples grown on some of the trees. They was yella apples, you know, my favorite. Sometimes I'd go pickin' one to eat, even though I wasn't s'posed to. Well, there was a ripe one hangin' pretty low, and I asked Miss Diamond if she wanted it, and she did. So I put her up on my shoulders so she could reach it herself. She almost had it when we heard ol' Mr. McMullen yellin' from the back porch.

"What the hell are you doin'?" he yelled. "You ain't s'posed to be out there with them!"

Now we were just confused because that's exactly what she *had* been doin' since she got there. Neither of us was gonna say that to 'im, though. So I got her down off my shoulders and put her down, and I said she'd better go on and get in the house.

"But I don't wanna go in there," she said.

"I know, Miss Diamond," I said, "but you don't wanna be makin' your daddy angry, now."

"He ain't my daddy," she said, but she went along back with her head down. She wasn't happy at all.

After that, she didn't come out much. She'd sit up on the back porch and look out at us, but she didn't dare come down. It sure dampened my spirits, though, but I figured it was the best. She was gonna be startin' school with the rest of the kids soon, so she wouldn't be out with us anyway. A few of the younger boys were gonna be gone, too, so just us older boys'd be out there every day. It was always a lonely time of the year, but I had figured that one would be even worse.

At the very end of August, August twenty-eighth to be exact, it was a Sunday. I remember it was the twenty-eighth because it was my eighteenth birthday. It was a Sunday, too, which is the only day of the week Mr. McMullen gave us off. I wasn't plannin' on doin' anything, and it was gonna be boss.

But then I had an idea. Because school was gonna be startin' in September, so there wasn't a whole lot of time when I'd be able to see my little friend. So I walked all the way over to the orchard around noontime because I knew they'd be home from church by then. It's a whole lot hotter walkin' there then than it is walkin' at dawn, I'll tell you what.

When I got there, I knocked on the front door, hopin' it wasn't Mr. McMullen who answered it. Thank God it was Mrs. McMullen. She asked me what I was doin' there on my day off, and I told her that today was my birthday, and I was wonderin' if Diamond wanted to hang around for the day since she was gonna be startin' school soon and all.

"Well, that's real sweet of you, Tom," she said. "I'll go and get her."

She went back in, and I heard some voices, including a man's voice, who was startin' to sound a little irritated. I prayed to God above that Mrs. McMullen hadn't been honest with him. That wouldn't be the last time I would wish that, neither.

The next person to open the door was Miss Diamond herself, still dressed in her Sunday clothes and her hair a mess like always. She came out in a hurry, grabbed my hand, and dragged me away.

"We gotta beat feet," she said. "'fore he changes his mind."

We ran all the way down the land and got movin' down the road. When we was far enough away, we slowed down a little, and I started laughin'.

"Miss Diamond," I said, "Do they even know you're gone?"

"Sure they do," she said. "He don't know where, but he don't care anyway."

"Good enough for me," I said.

So we went on walkin' a few miles down the road to my home. I used to live in a little wooden house that my daddy built in '37, just 'fore I was born. It's just a straight shot down from the orchard, though they mighta tore it down now. It was a good walk from the orchard, but Miss Diamond never complained about it once.

When we got there, I opened the door and let her inside. She went lookin' around and all, not that there's a whole lot to look at. The whole house was two rooms, all wood. There was a kitchen area with a sink basin and a couple of cheap appliances in the back corner of the main room. My daddy had two chairs and a table sittin' in there. On the other side, two rockin' chairs was sittin' next to his radio and a little table to set a beer on or somethin'. There used to be two beds in the other room, now there's only the one in there, with a little chest of drawers. Everywhere in the house, I had all types of things taped up on the walls. Pictures out of the newspaper, pictures of my mamma and daddy, clippin's about all kinds of things goin' on in the news, and all sorts of other things that were my daddy's.

The most of any one thing I had up on the walls was my daddy's collection. He rigged a bunch of them guns up there, just to display 'em when he wasn't usin' 'em. He used to care a whole lot about how they was lookin'; he'd take 'em down and clean 'em all the time. When he died back in '45, I took it upon myself to keep them lookin' alright. I think a lot about if somebody's gone and taken 'em while I've been away.

Breaks my heart to think about my daddy. They came and brought me some of his things when he died over there, and mamma was gone, but no one bothered to come and take me away from there, and that was the way I liked it. I'd been livin' in that old house alone for eleven years by the time Miss Diamond was there.

Miss Diamond had only been lookin' around for a moment when she said to me, "You live here alone." Again, she never asked because she knew already.

"I sure do," I said.

She said, "You're an orphan, too."

I said, "Yes."

"But you didn't tell me that," she said.

"Well," I said, "you know, it ain't everything. A person with no parents can be a whole lot of other things, too. He ain't just an orphan all the time. Just like you's a whole lot more'n a little girl with one arm, you know."

She thought about that, and then she looked up at the back wall where most of the collection was. "You have a lot of guns," she said.

"They was my daddy's," I said. "He liked to collect 'em. I don't even know where he got some of 'em."

"What did he do with them?" she asked me.

"Well, most of 'em were for huntin'," I said. "He'd go and catch some dinner and bring it back for us to eat. It wasn't always the best of things, but we ate. And that's what mattered."

Then she asked me, "how long have they been gone?"

"Oh," I said, "'bout ten years now. Mamma died while Daddy was fightin' in the war, then he died, too. He didn't even know she was gone. But I'll tell you what, come take a look at this." I went into the bedroom and got my favorite gun outta the drawer. I didn't keep it with the others because I thought that if anybody came and wanted to steal the collection, they'd be more'n satisfied with the guns on the wall. But this was one I never wanted anything to happen to.

I brought it back out to her and held it out. "This here's a Victory Model," I said. "Smith and Wesson. My daddy had it with him in Europe. They brought it back to me with the rest of his things when he died. They usually wouldn't do that, s'pose one of them officers knew he was a collector and smuggled it for me."

Miss Diamond looked at it like it was gonna explode. I guess she'd never held a gun before.

"You can hold it," I said. "It can't hurt ya. It ain't even loaded."

So she took it. I almost started laughin' because she held it like it was gonna break or somethin'. She looked at it for a while, then she held it back up to me.

"You wanna see it in action?" I asked her. She said sure, although she seemed a little worried, poor thing. But I told her I wasn't gonna let nothin' bad happen to her, and she knew it already. And I sure meant it.

So I grabbed a clip from the same drawer, and we went outside, walkin' around to the back. She was stood right next to me because she wanted to see how it worked. I showed her me puttin' the clip in and turnin' the safety off.

"Now, this here's a double-action," I told her, "So I don't have to pull the hammer back to turn the wheel to get a new bullet in there. All I have to do is pull the trigger." Then I told her she might wanna cover her ears and step back a little. She just looked me in the face, blinked, and held up her one hand. She was so tough sometimes, I'd forget she was crippled.

"Well, how about this," I said. "You stand on this side, put your hand on the one ear, and I'll put my hand on the other."

So we did that. I put my hand on her ear, trying not to push too hard but makin' sure it was covered. Then I aimed the gun down at a big tree yonder with my other hand and pulled the trigger. The bullet scratched up the bark in the exact spot I was aimin' for. I'm a damn good shot, but most know that already now. Don't feel uncomfortable, now, Detective. I'm just bein' plain with ya, is all.

After the shot, I looked over at Miss Diamond and took my hand off her ear. She was just lookin' down at the tree with these wide eyes. I smiled and turned the safety on.

"Can I try it?" she asked me.

"Naw, Miss Diamond," I said. "Your daddy wouldn't like that, and you know it. It's bad enough you're here with me at all."

She said, "Will you stop callin' him that? He ain't my daddy, and he never will be, neither."

I said, "You don't like him all that much, do ya?" She nodded. "What about Mrs. McMullen? Do you like her?"

"She's alright," she said. "She gets mad at me, though. But she only gets mad when he's mad, too. I don't like that she uses my middle name when she's mad."

That made me laugh. "You got a middle name?" I asked her.

"Well, sure," she said. "Don't everyone?"

"Most, I think," I said. "What's yours?"

"What's *yours*?" She asked me.

I laughed again. Remember when I said Miss Diamond didn't say too much? It's because she never wanted to. She'd always be yellin' at me for askin' her questions. I wonder how her teachers got on with her before, well, 'fore she left.

I gave in to her because I knew she'd tell me if I told her first. "My middle name's Peter," I said. "It was my daddy's name. I'm Thomas Peter."

"You sure loved your daddy," she said.

"Only 'cause he loved me," I said. "I was lucky, I know that. Now quit stallin', what's your middle name?"

She sighed and rolled her eyes at me. "Rose," she said. "Diamond Rose."

"Well, ain't that a pretty name," I said. "Nice to meet ya, Miss Diamond Rose."

"Please, don't start callin' me that," she said.

"I won't," I said. Then I asked her, "You scared about schoolin'?"

"I ain't scared," she said, but that look on her face said somethin' different.

"It's okay to be nervous, you know," I said. "I'm sure it ain't easy."

"You ever been to school?" She asked me.

"Naw," I said.

"That ain't fair, Tom!" She said. "Why do I have to go?"

"Because ol' Mr. and Mrs. McMullen is sendin' ya," I said, laughin'. "Sometimes kids don't get a choice. Does that make you unhappy?"

She took a second before answerin'. "No more'n usual," she said. "I'm unhappy all the time. Happiest I've been is spendin' time with you."

"Well," I said, "I'm happy spendin' time with you, too."

Now, I'd never thought of me havin' a happy life. You're probably thinkin' me, and Miss Diamond's the same for that. I might've agreed with you. But just then, when she was talkin' to me, I realized that while I mighta been tryna keep floatin' all my life, she was sittin' at the bottom of the ocean with sharks hoverin' over her. And she didn't see the point of tryin' to get out because she was in too deep. She had never even seen the light of the sun. I never tried to make her feel like she was down there, but she already knew, just like always.

We were just standin' there, in the little clearin' behind my house, lookin' out into the trees. She stared at that tree I'd shot for a second, and I wondered for a second, well, I wondered if she was jealous of it. You know, that little girl had a habit of makin' me remember my heart was intact, just in time to break it.

Then she said, "I think I'm always gonna be unhappy."

And I said, "Well, you ain't the first. And I gotta feelin' you won't be the last, Diamond Rose."

* * *

~ 9 ~

LADY TROUBLES

09:30 AM.

Banks' head was whirling by the time the guard tapped the glass. Every visit held more and more to decipher, and this one was the biggest of all. The first thing she thought was the gun checked out, not that she was expecting otherwise. He had already included that detail in his testimony, so it was to be expected that he would spin that into the story somewhere.

Oh, yes, the Victory Model. Banks had done her research on the firearm before. It had been a commonly used sidearm for the United States during the Second World War and other allied countries, most notably Great Britain. All the details of this .38 revolver were in the case file. It was a classic Smith and Wesson, once used for the good of the USA from 1942 to 1945, later used in 1955 to murder two men in a private barn.

There were more details now, of course. Banks was under orders not to tell Tom Higgins this: that exact firearm had been found, just two months earlier, two states over in a Louisiana bayou.

According to the young man who found it, the safety had been on, with two rounds missing, leaving four. Forensically, upon analysis, no fingerprints could be detected, which was not surprising. It had been there for a very long time; they estimated approximately eight to ten years. The serial number and rounds present only tied the possible criminal use of the firearm to be attached to this case.

Tom sat and watched as Banks collected her notes and herself and got ready to leave again. He didn't have any closing remarks like he usually did, and she wondered if he finally spent his energy from this longer-than-normal session. But when she asked the question she had been sitting on, he still looked chipper as ever when he answered her.

"Whatever happened to that firearm, Tom?" Banks asked. She knew the answer, but she wanted to hear what he would say. Just as she expected, he stuck to his previous answer.

"I threw it away on that night," he said with no hesitation. "I don't remember where, and I don't know what happened after. They still ain't found it?"

"No," Banks lied. "They haven't found it yet."

"They still lookin'?" He asked.

This one was not a lie. "Not anymore."

He smiled a little, and Banks wondered if it was the gun he was worried about.

"Figured," he said. "Wasn't important enough, I guess."

"I guess not," she said. "Personally, I'd have liked to see it. The history, and all."

Tom smiled wider at her. "I wish you could have, Detective. That's a beautiful weapon." His smile faltered, and he looked down.

Banks was concerned her effort to cover her tracks had been too apparent, so she shifted the conversation.

"You said your middle name was 'Peter,'" Banks recalled. "After your father. But there was no middle name included in the court report. Why is that?"

He smiled at her. "It was the one thing they let me have," he said. "I asked them to leave the middle name out of it."

"How come?" She asked.

"Well," he answered, "Guess I didn't want his name attached to what I did. I know he'd be real disappointed."

Banks was unsure how to respond, so she just nodded politely at him with an empathetic smile. Then she stood up and left him there in his thoughts.

So the gun used for murder in Dothan, Alabama, was found in the Louisiana bayou, ten years after the crime occurred. Could it have been stolen from its original hiding spot, as Tom had said, and passed along until it ended up in the swamp?

It was certainly possible, but Banks was more inclined to believe that a specific runaway had taken it away when she left. And Banks knew precisely why. If the relationship, spun by Tom in his stories, was accurate to real life, it would make complete sense for Diamond to want to take the gun, thinking that lack of evidence would save her friend from his fate. She likely would not have known about the other forms of evidence that could convict him, even without the weapon present.

Now, the question was this: did Tom know that Diamond had taken the gun at all? His tone when he asked if the gun was still being searched for suggested that he did, and the thing he wanted to know about was whether Diamond herself had been found or the whereabouts of them both. If that was *really* what he was wondering, then there were a few scenarios to explore:

1. The first was that because Tom knew that Diamond had the gun, and his concerns lie with them conjoined with each other. If the firearm concerned him, the main question was, 'why?' He had already confessed to using the weapon, so the evidence provided by it in that sense was unneeded. But what if more findings were sitting with that weapon? If there were, Banks would have known them already, so what could he be worried about?

2. The second scenario Banks considered was this: if the girl and the gun *are* together, perhaps Tom was concerned about Diamond being found with it at all. Maybe they would charge her

with accessory and send her to juvenile, yet another unfeeling institution. Tom surely would not have wanted that for her.

3. It was also possible that his concerns could lie with both of them in separation, even if they were together. It could be that he genuinely wanted to know if his father's gun had been found and was now in safe hands and expressed the same concern for the girl. Perhaps he simply wondered where his friend was and if she was happy?

Any of these situations were possible, not to mention the possibility that was the current belief, that Diamond had run away and never been found, and the gun had been haphazardly thrown away and stolen and turned up years later, while its owner remained in prison. As Banks was driving back up to Montgomery in her old '54 Chevy Bel-Air, she set her mind adrift in the sea of possibilities submerging the events that followed the night of September 21, 1955.

THURSDAY, AUGUST 5, 1965. 10:13 AM.

Many moments in history serve as catastrophic, though inevitable, changes in course for people worldwide. D-Day on Normandy Beach in 1945, the rise and fall of the Roman Empire, boxes of tea thrown overboard in Boston in 1773, and the subsequent Revolutionary war that killed thousands on both sides. Even as recent as Bloody Sunday, a horrific event following the civil rights march from Selma to Montgomery, which, though tragic and unnecessarily violent, set in motion progress in its own way.

All of these examples, Banks decided, paled in comparison to *that* moment. The moment she felt both the overwhelming betrayal of what was happening and the burning realization, it was inevitable.

"You're *pulling the case*?" She asked, flabbergasted, as she stood up from her seat across the desk from Sgt. Nichols, who was not shy to reveal his not-so-secret glee upon seeing her reaction to this news. He reeled in said glee only to express disappointment at her behavior.

"Now, doll," he patronized, "I told you before that this was going to happen if there was no progress. It's been two weeks, and you still have nothing to report."

"I told you what I found," she responded, still standing. "And I've been working on other cases in the meantime. Sarge, you have to admit there are holes in this story! Why wouldn't Higgins want the gun to be discovered if there was nothing additional to be found on it? Was Diamond McMullen a witness? Did she run away by her own accord, or did she take the gun on purpose, and what *was* that purpose? We have a motive for the murder of Alan Holt, but he was supposed to be coincidental. And maybe Tom killed them, sure, but no one seems to care that it might have been self-defense, just because of the circumstances leading up to it! And we *know* now that there are definitive lies in his testimony. Tom's still hiding more, Sarge. He knows *more*, and he hasn't told anyone, but *why*?"

"*I don't know, and I don't give a good God damn!*" Sgt. Nichols rose from his chair as he raised his voice in response to Banks' ramblings. "Higgins is in jail for the next twenty years for murders *he* committed. Nothing he has to say matters now! He can rot in that cell forever for all I care because he's *guilty*! *What is the point* of diggin' into this anymore, Detective?"

Banks had more fight left in her, but she still did not want to lose her job. She took a risk and responded.

"I wish you would trust me enough to continue this," she said, trying to keep an even tone. "You would never do this to Wild, or Boris, or Jameson, or Karp. You only do this shit to me, and I just can't understand why you can't let me have this."

"It ain't me, Detective," he said, still stern but no longer yelling. "It's them up there. The Captain himself said it was pointless to continue, and I agree."

Banks sighed. "Fine," she said. She would normally wait to be dismissed, but she turned and began to leave when the Sergeant stopped her.

"Detective," he said, and she turned back to look at him. "You ever think that this fight you're givin' ain't about Higgins, ain't about the case? Maybe you're just fightin' because you want someone to see you and give you a chance. Well, I'm here to tell you that you can hope and pray for a chance all you want, but if you keep spending all your time on nonsense, maybe you'd be better off working a front desk somewhere."

"No, sir," she said. "Not me."

"Well, then," he said. "Maybe you should take a long weekend to think about how you wanna come back to work and do cases that matter. When you come back Monday, I expect you to be on your game if you're gonna stay. You can leave your gun and badge, too."

Banks had never felt lower. Her chest was hollow, and she felt like she couldn't breathe. Her rage was replaced with the pain from the dagger he'd thrust into her heart. She barely felt like responding, but she used everything she had to get the last word as she set her badge and gun on his desk.

"Yes, *sir.*"

FRIDAY, AUGUST 6, 1965. 08:14 AM.

Banks still felt so drained the next day after the conversation in the Sergeant's office.

Now, it was a Friday, and Banks had woken up that morning and immediately reminded herself that she had nowhere to be. Instead of staying home feeling sorry for herself, she decided to do the opposite of what everyone else seemingly wanted her to do: whatever she damn well felt like. Today, even after the blow of the terminated case, she had only one person she wanted to see.

Banks' old Bel-Air pulled up at the Dothan Penitentiary at eight o'clock on the dot, and Banks emerged with steadfast determination. When she reached the front desk inside, she told the older woman who was always sitting there that she intended to speak to Mr. Tom Higgins that morning.

"They didn't tell me you were coming," she said. "Was this a planned visit?"

Banks felt a rush of impatience but kept it in with a lot of effort.

"No," she said. "I hadn't been sure if my schedule would allow me to visit this morning, but as it turned out, I have time. Is it a problem that I showed up impromptu? I can't imagine Mr. Higgins has many appointments to attend to."

Banks surprised herself with the confidence she oozed and the ease she felt in lying to this woman for what was essentially her own gain.

"Well," the woman said, increasingly uncomfortable with the disorganization of Banks' visit. "They do like things to be scheduled in advance, erm, *Detective*." Banks did not like how this woman said 'Detective,' like it did not fit correctly in her mouth. "I'll see what I can do."

Before she could do anything more, a correctional officer appeared behind the woman, laid eyes on Banks, and immediately recognized the situation. "Ah, Detective Banks," he said, an amused tone to his voice. "Your Sergeant called earlier, notifying us that you would no longer be visiting Mr. Higgins. I'm sure you just came down to let us know."

Banks met the confused and surprised eyes of the woman behind the desk and felt nothing but guilt.

"Yes," Banks said, "that's why I came down. I hadn't realized he had contacted you already."

"Long drive from Montgomery," the officer said. "Sorry about your luck." He grabbed a paper off the desk and started to walk away before turning back and offering a sarcastic, "Hang loose, Detective."

Banks herself also turned to leave, seeing now that her investigation was truly over when the office lady piped up behind her desk.

"You *could* come back as a visitor," she called after Banks. "I could try to schedule you next week. Available times are only once a week, but it's something."

Banks smiled with gratitude. "That would be lovely, thank you."

"Of course!" The woman said, writing something down on a piece of paper. "It's clear you enjoy seeing him."

"Oh?" Banks asked, still smiling.

"Sure!" The older woman smiled as she continued writing and then put the paper to the side. "Can't say I've ever seen something like that happen. But Ripley, oh, I mean, the guard who shows you in, says Mr. Higgins is always pleased as punch on days you come to talk to him."

"Ah-hah," Banks said, finally understanding and almost laughing at the insinuation. "Lovely. Well, thank you!"

"Not a problem, dear," the woman said, waving to Banks. "I'll be sure to have him put in the *private* cell again, don't you worry!"

Banks wasn't the biggest fan of the circumstances that the woman in the penitentiary had invented up for Banks and Tom Higgins in her mind, but she supposed that either way, it was good that she would be able to speak to him again.

That was her least favorite part about being a woman; the number of boxes you are kept in and prevented from leaving. The default script of a woman's life that no woman could escape without a fight, a fight which she could never win or lose without consequences. No one would expect a *woman* to want to visit a *prisoner* for the sake of her career in investigative work. No, she *had* to be in love with him. Even worse still, because Banks was born in this world and was accustomed to its quirks, she wondered if it was, indeed, a proper perspective.

You do *like his company,* she thought, *and you* have *been sympathetic to his story, having had no such sympathy for others in similar standings.*

She rolled her eyes in response to her thoughts. Even if she *did* feel anything like that for Tom Higgins, which she didn't, it wouldn't matter. He was a criminal and a murderer, and she would never stoop so low for something so trivial as love.

But then what if he's not a criminal? she thought. *Does wondering something like that imply that I do feel for him? Can my intuition be that good? Is that what this is? Am I questioning this seemingly straightforward case because my instinct is kicking in, or is it just plain wishful thinking?*

Banks didn't feel like going home. She did not even want to be in the same city as Sgt. Nichols, or the station, or any of it. After sitting awhile and considering her plans, she decided to take a drive down memory lane. Though, admittedly, not her own.

09:02 AM.

Dothan, Alabama was a charming town, and the people walking around downtown all looked to be in good spirits. Banks parked her car and walked around. However, she was not too frivolous in her travels because she had a mission to accomplish during this visit. Banks actively tried to make this excursion feel as much like police work as possible, despite having no badge, no firearm, and no support.

After looking around downtown Dothan for a while, Banks stood at the corner of Foster and Main in front of Blumberg's Department Store. Looking up the street, she could see signs for several sweet-looking stores in brick buildings, as well as a giant vertical sign for a theater just a block or two away. There were many people around, though Banks figured there would be many more when it was not working hours.

Banks asked a couple of people passing by if they knew where the McMullen orchard was. Everyone she asked made a point to tell her that the orchard wasn't called 'McMullen' anymore.

"It got bought up years ago," they all said. "It's called Hale and Pritchett now."

Upon repetition of her original question, only a couple of the people gave her directions worth anything. She took the information she collected and drove where they told her to. After a few turns, one of which was wrong on her account, she finally reached a country road, either side of which was nothing but farmland and trees. She figured she had probably made it to the right road, just in time to see trees in the distance.

As she got closer, she could see a fence stretching back at least a couple miles, and beyond it stood row after row of apple trees, some of which had spots of yellow visible already. Some other fruit trees were in another block behind that, and closest to Banks coming from the left was a reddish-brown barn. In front of the orchard was a long, dirt lane leading to a two-story, sky blue country house with white trim. The porch wrapped around all sides of it, and the yard was well kept and green. The front garden was lush, with beautiful flowers on either side of the front porch steps leading to the door.

Banks drove up the lane and eventually parked her Bel-Air in the gravel driveway right out front, admiring the view all the way. It was ideal and romantic, the picture of rural perfection. There were so many white-trimmed windows that Banks wondered if there was any wall space inside at all. She had only been sitting in the drive for a few minutes when a young woman in a yellow sundress came out the front door and waved at her. She immediately felt embarrassed for sitting there so long.

Emerging from the driver's seat, Banks waved back at the woman and called a greeting. The woman smiled a little and started down the stairs. Banks met the woman halfway up the stone walkway leading to the stairs.

"Hello," the young woman said, still smiling. She had reddish-blonde hair and freckled cheeks. She could not have been more than twenty, Banks figured. "How can I help ya?"

Banks immediately faltered. She wasn't sure if she should be honest or if it would be better to lie. Especially if the woman called up the chain to check her sources, Banks could be in deep if she wasn't careful. She decided that she would be truthful about her intentions, kind of, but would conveniently forget to mention that she was from Montgomery or working on a case she shouldn't be.

"Well, this is a little embarrassing," she said, thinking fast. "I am actually down this way because I'm gathering information for a practice case." *Where are we going with this, Isla?* "I'm trying to become a detective, and so they assigned us old cases to research for an examination." *Not your best, but keep going.* "My case is a murder case that occurred here in 1955 if you're familiar with it. The Higgins case?"

The young woman went from a sunny smile to swallowing nervously. "Oh, yes," she said. "Tom Higgins. He killed my daddy."

"Oh, my!" Banks exclaimed, immediately pulling out of character, bewildered. "I'm sorry, I thought the property was under different owners now. Color me embarrassed. So that must make you—?"

"Oh, where are my manners?" She said, laughing nervously. "I'm Imogen, Imogen McMullen. Well, Pritchett, now. My husband bought the property from my mamma a couple of years back." She held out a hand. "Most people call me Idg—"

"Idgie," Banks said, shaking her hand and feeling a little like she was meeting a character from a storybook. "Of course, one of the twins."

Idgie looked a little more at ease for being recognized. Her smile seemed a little more genuine, and she let out a sigh that she appeared to be suppressing a little. "Yes, that's right," she said. "The other twin's usually here, but she had some errands in town today."

"That's quite alright," Banks said, relieved that Idgie didn't seem upset by her second impromptu visit that day. "Well, I didn't mean to intrude. I'll go if you want me to."

"Oh, no," Idgie said, any discomfort fading away and swiftly replaced by deep-set Southern hospitality. "Please stick around if you want to. I could show you around back; I'm sure you mighta heard of the barn and all. You could get a little tour or somethin'?"

Banks didn't want to be too eager, but she could not resist the offer.

"That would be lovely," she said.

~ 10 ~

NO PLACE LIKE HOME

As Idgie Pritchett showed Isla Banks around the Hale and Pritchett Orchard, Banks tried to remember every detail she had gotten
from Tom's story up to that point. As she looked around, she tried
to picture the events taking place in the actual setting, now that it
was right there in front of her.

They strolled around the house, and Banks could see the back of
the porch. She imagined little Diamond McMullen sitting up there,
waiting for the boys to come around. Banks could see through her
own eyes what Tom would have seen every day, walking around
and out to where the trees began, healthy and green and well-
tended. It was a vast stretch of land, even when the trees stopped,
the fence around the property just kept going, and as Banks stared
into the distance, she thought of Tom Higgins and Miss Diamond
sitting on the fence, talking about their lives and struggles, finding
real friendship for the first time in their young lives.

Banks knew that Idgie might have been thinking of similar
things, but they weren't rose-colored the way Banks' imaginings
were. If she thought of Tom Higgins, she only thought of the bastard
who killed her father and disgraced her mother. She might have
thought of Diamond, but she only would have known how weird she
might have thought the girl was and additionally how strange her
disappearance was.

"Well, here it is," Idgie said with her arms out to the orchard, the two of them standing at the edge of the apple trees, smelling the sweet aroma of summer and feeling the Alabama sun and boiling humidity. It was sweltering outside, and Banks was thankful she had decided to ditch the blazer today. Even so, the view was worth the constant sweat.

"This place is beautiful," Banks said.

"Well, I thank ya," Idgie said. "This here's been my home all my life. I do try to keep it goin' the way it always did. Ain't got much help from the family, but I got Dolly and our husbands. They're the 'Hale,' in Hale and Pritchett, of course. Dolly's pregnant too; she's gonna have a baby boy!"

Now that Banks knew this was the same Idgie from the Mc-Mullen story, she knew the twins would be nineteen now, and she could thank traditional values for the both of them being married so soon in life. She knew, however, that as long as they were happy, it was none of her concern.

"You're both here?" Banks asked. "You must be very close."

"Always were," Idgie said with a charming smile. "We're twins, after all. Ain't much closer we could get. When Johnnie bought the orchard, and we started gettin' acquainted, I was plannin' to stay here, of course, and the house is big enough for two families, so she stayed behind, too. I'm glad to have her here, too. I don't know what I'd do without her."

Banks felt a tinge of familiarity. "Did you say, 'Johnnie?'"

"Yes, ma'am," Idgie said, "that's my husband."

"Johnnie *Pritchett*?" Banks asked. "The one who used to work here?"

"Well, you sure have done your research," Idgie laughed. "Yes, ma'am, the very same. And he *still does* work here, too, that's for sure!"

Banks found herself smiling along with Idgie like she had been a friend of the family for years. "How did he manage that?" She asked.

"Well," Idgie said, speaking much more freely for having a friendly audience, "His mamma and daddy died around the time Mamma was thinkin' of sellin'. Johnnie was still here, you know. He'd sneak me a lookin' every so often, too, that boy. He was worried about losin' his job when it got sold, and the other boys, too. So when his mamma and daddy left him some money, instead of hittin' the road, he negotiated a price with Mamma. She was real desperate to sell, you know, and I was tellin' her I knew he'd take care of the orchard. Things went on from there, you know, the boys kept their jobs, and we can even afford to pay them a good workin' wage. Johnnie's just about livin' his dream, bless his heart."

Banks could see the pride in Idgie's freckled face, and she found herself feeling the same.

"Far out!" Banks said, remembering Tom's story about when he fought Tuck in Johnnie's sister's barn, thinking how if she had been able to go back in time and tell Johnnie he would own the orchard one day, he would definitely think she was smoking grass or something. "I can only imagine how proud he must be."

Idgie looked appreciative of Banks' empathetic exclamation. "Oh, he's over the moon. Mamma gave him a good deal since he worked here so long."

"Where is she now?" Banks asked, hoping the answer wouldn't dampen spirits.

Luckily, Idgie responded with a smile and an eye roll, implying something was off about the situation, but not tragic, at least. "Oh, she's around. Don't live here anymore, but she comes by all the time to check on things, you know how mammas are. No, she lives over in Enterprise. Betty, too. Oh—" Idgie trailed off and sighed, having hit a memory. "Poor Betty. She couldn't stand stayin' around here any longer. No, she moved out and got herself another life.

"She visits every so often, though," Idgie interrupted herself to reassure that portion of the story. "She's still family, and she's got her own family, too. She's a Miller, now. Husband and kids, kids we never see. Can't imagine why, but I think she might be ashamed of us."

"Oh, I'm sure that's not it," Banks said, as though reassuring a close friend. "She just is caught up in her own thing like people do. I'm sure she'll come around."

"Oh, yeah," Idgie said. "Yeah, the rest of 'em's out on their own, too. Rodney's been travellin' around Europe an' all. I don't even know where he's at now. Last we heard, he was somewhere in France. But that was months ago, now. And Billy," Idgie chuckled a little. "Well, he goes by 'William' now. He's away at school, up in New York, of all places. I'm worried he's not gonna come back down; that's a whole new world up there, you know. But as long as he's happy, I guess."

"Well," Banks said, trying to offer a little reassurance, "At least you have Dolly, and Betty's still nearby in the state, at least. She looked after you kids years ago, didn't she? I'm sure if you needed anything, she'd come back."

"I sure hope so," Idgie said. "Poor thing. You'd've thought she died that night." Idgie looked to her left at the barn, which sat there with its own energy like it was watching them. Then she turned to look at Banks and nodded her head towards it. "You wanna see it?"

Again, Banks withheld herself from the eagerness burning her insides.

"I would," she said, "if that's alright."

Idgie led Banks over to the massive barn, and again Banks tried to imagine the events of days past. Except these memories had no rosy tint to keep them fresh. They were rotten, waiting in the dark and hiding things from the light of day.

Idgie opened the door for Banks to go inside and then the other door to let light inside. The cavernous rafters loomed above them, making them feel very small. The slatted walls inside were the same reddish-brown as the outside, and loose hay covered the floor. For a moment, Banks thought she saw a spot of blood but was unable to find it again. There were glimmers of light coming through the wood, and she wondered if they had ever fixed the loose slat in the back Tom had told her about. There were no animals in the barn. But if there were, would they know why this feeling hung in the air?

Before she could say anything about the feeling, Idgie stood next to her and took the words right out of her mouth.

"It's a little colder in here, ain't it?" She asked.

"It sure is," Banks confirmed. It *was*, too. Shade could not shelter you from Alabama humidity, but in here, Banks felt a different something suspended in the air. They stood there without speaking, but there was a feeling of constant noise, not heard but undoubtedly felt.

"Sometimes I think I see someone come in here," Idgie said, clearly uncomfortable but remaining very calm. "When I'm just in the house or workin' outside. Then I come over and open the door, and ain't no one in here. I know it's silly, but it always looks like Daddy."

It's just a barn, Banks thought, as a tingle ran up and down her spine. *You've seen fresh crime scenes and senseless violence beyond what occurred here. There are no ghosts. There's nothing to be afraid of. This suffocating feeling is not because of apparitions or any of that hocus pocus.*

"Huh," Banks allowed, not sure how else to respond, and then she suddenly felt herself return to her senses. "Thank you for showing me. We don't have to stay in here if you don't want to."

Idgie looked around one last time and nodded. The two of them left as soon as they had come in, and Idgie closed the doors behind them.

"I should say also," Banks said. "I'm sorry about what happened to your father."

Idgie dismissed the sentiment. "It was a long while ago," she said. "Long time."

They stood in silence for a moment, each inside their head, unsure how to continue. Banks wondered if she should leave when something occurred to Idgie.

"In your research," she said, "have you spoken to him? To Tom?"

Banks was again unsure what the least harmful thing to say was, but the thing that came the most naturally was the truth.

"Yes," she said. "Yes, I have."

Idgie shifted a bit and bit her lip. "Are you plannin' on talkin' to him more?"

"Yes," Banks said. "I am."

Idgie almost looked disappointed, not because of a distaste of Banks' chosen conversation partner, but for a different reason. It seemed she had something that had been sitting in her mind for a while that she had wanted to get out but was not sure if she was ready.

"Well, when you see him," she said, "Tell him I forgive him."

Idgie's statement was not at all what Banks expected, and it frustrated the ongoing conflict in her mind even more than it had already been.

"You do?" She asked. "After what he did?"

"Well, sure," she said, standing steadier now that she had gotten the first part out of her system. "I know Tom killed my daddy and the other boy, too. I didn't know why, and I still don't, I guess. I was only nine, and things were kept from me at the time that I know now. I know he got with Mamma, and that was hard to hear, of course. But I also know that if he hadn't've killed Daddy, then Daddy might've killed *him*, and I honestly don't know which one is worse."

Banks was caught between herself again. Here was a child of a murder victim, and even *she* accepted that there was potential self-defense at play when Tom Higgins pulled the trigger (Banks could not help but recognize that this sensible explanation was coming from another woman and found herself not in the least bit surprised). She wanted to explore this more with Idgie, but at the same time, she knew that Idgie had allowed herself to come to this conclusion while Tom was in prison, after a significant amount of time had passed. If Banks went on about how Tom wasn't as guilty as people decided he was, she could trigger an adverse reaction in Idgie. She could not ignore this, but how far could she push?

"Well," Banks began, delicately, "you know he's serving thirty years. If you believe it was self-defense, he might be able to get less."

"I was nine," Idgie said. "I was in Betty's room with everybody else when it happened. I don't know what happened, and I don't know what to believe."

Banks had pretty much known what Idgie would say before she said it, so she let herself take a breath and move on.

"Speaking of everyone else," she said, changing the subject just a bit. "Just for the sake of asking, did you know Diamond was planning on running away?"

Banks saw a tear form in Idgie's eye, and she immediately took her foot off the gas.

"I'm sorry," she said quickly. "I didn't mean to push; you don't have to answer. It was just curiosity."

Idgie smiled a little and let the tear fall from her eye before wiping it from her cheek. "It's alright," she reassured, laughing just a little at herself. "Ain't your fault it happened. I was never really that close with Diamond, but I sure feel guilty about how we treated her. I was just a kid, but I should've known better." She wiped another fresh tear from her cheek and sniffed. "That's the other thing about Tom I could never understand. How could a man who cared so much about that poor girl have the poor sense to go messin' around and killin' people?"

How indeed, Banks thought.

"I don't know," Banks said. "I'm trying to figure that out, myself."

11:32 AM.

After a little more looking around, Banks bid Idgie Pritchett farewell at around eleven-thirty and drove away. However, instead of turning right to go back the way she came, she turned left to go elsewhere. She hoped the little bit of direction she had would lead her there.

After about two miles, the fields ended, and there was a shady stretch of road with trees on both sides. There were no other cars around, so Banks drove slowly, carefully searching for any openings in the woods. Finally, she came across a gap in the brush on her left, so narrow she almost drove right past it. She pulled over on the side of the road and got out, checking both ways before crossing to the opening. There was just a small path leading into the wood, and as Banks stepped along it, making fast friends with a few mosquitos, she began to see a structure hidden by greenery.

There it is, she thought.

Indeed, sitting amidst the overgrown trees and shrubbery was a little wooden cabin with just one door and two small windows in the front. The path led directly up to two steps leading up to the door, and Banks laughed a little at the thought that if she did not know whose house this was, it would feel like a trap. At least the house wasn't made of candy.

Banks continued up the path, still not moving too fast, though why not, she was not sure. When she reached the door, she examined the knob, which did have a lock above it, though there were many scratch marks around it, as though someone had tried, perhaps successfully, to pick the lock. She put a hand on her side where her gun should have been, then remembered upon feeling nothing that Sgt. Nichols had requested she leave her gun at the station until she came back to work on Monday. Feeling increasingly vulnerable, she decided that the simplest way to know if anyone was inside without making them feel threatened was to knock on the door.

Knock knock. No answer. Banks tried it again, still no response. She called, "Hello?" Nothing. She then figured either there was no one inside, or they were waiting for her to try the door. Regardless of her temporary civilian status at that moment, she tried one last time to excite any trespassers. "Montgomery Police, open the door, please!" She called, and still nothing. For her pride, she looked around, partly to make sure no one was stalking her movements but also to make sure they hadn't seen her calling to no one.

Alright, she thought. *Let's go in.*

She tried the knob, and it turned. Figuring whoever had picked the lock had left with the door unlocked (or just never tried the knob), she proceeded to enter. The door opened to a small living space that perfectly matched Tom's description, from the basin sink in the kitchen corner to the rocking chairs to the pictures covering the walls floor to ceiling. There, to the left, was an open door leading into a small bedroom with only a bed and a dresser. The only thing that was missing, which made Banks' heart involuntarily plummet, was the collection.

Even without Tom's description, it was clear where they should have been, because the nails and hooks that once held them were still all over the back wall, and in some spots, the wood had aged around where they stayed all those years, leaving crisp marks in the shape of guns imprinted there. Banks was just wondering if she should tell Tom they were gone the next time she saw him when a glint on the kitchen table to her left caught her eye.

She turned her head to look over to the little round table, and the only thing sitting on it was a small revolver. She furrowed her brow and crossed over to it slowly, checking around corners as she did so. She did not pick it up but sat at one of the kitchen chairs, leaning in to examine it. It was a Smith and Wesson, too, but not a Victory model like Peter Higgins' war pistol. Banks didn't know enough about Smith and Wesson to know anything more about this specific model, but she knew enough to know it was old enough to have belonged to Tom's father, but it showed no sign of dust, so it could not have been sitting there long.

Come to think of it, Banks thought, *the table isn't dusty either.*

As Banks went to look around at the other furniture to search for dust, she caught movement out of the corner of her eye, out of the only other window in the house, just above the kitchen table. She stood, looking out the window and instinctively putting her hand to her side, just to once again be frustrated by coming up empty. She considered taking the revolver, but after about a minute of looking out the window and seeing nothing except the clearing and more trees, she took in a breath and looked around her in the house, seeing nothing in there either.

Great, she thought. *Now I'm seeing ghosts.*

09:17 PM.

After a surprisingly eventful trip to Dothan that morning, Isla Banks found herself back in her Montgomery apartment that evening, laying on her couch and staring up at the ceiling.

Banks' apartment was quaint but minimalistic and orderly. Both the couch she laid on and the recliner chair to the right of it were olive green and rayon tweed, setting in an earthy tone along with the chestnut walls and walnut, square basket hardwood floors. Against one wall, opposite to the recliner and under a window, which offered a view of the brick wall of a neighboring building, was a roll-top desk, neatly organized and polished. The desk was in uniform tone to the wooden end tables at either end of the couch, which were, in turn, consistent with the flooring. The walls had minimal hangings, including one modest, circular mirror hanging above the couch and two earth-toned landscapes on either side of it, all of which Banks purchased at Loveman's Department store. There were multiple books stored on the shelves of the desk, as well as on the end tables and the window sill. One might enter this apartment and think it simple or bland, but Isla Banks knew that when taking the books into account, that apartment held whole worlds.

She had made herself a small dinner in her tiny kitchen with the same color scheme as the rest of the house, the leftovers of which were sitting on her green and yellow metal tray coffee table. She had turned her square, wooden television set on, intending to watch it but having yet to even glance at the screen.

Banks thought until she could almost smell smoke coming from her head. It was only when a reporter on the news said something that caught her attention that she tore herself away from the day and sat up to watch:

"Today, August 6th, 1965, President Lyndon Johnson signed off on what is being called the 'Voting Rights Act,' which is being put in place to ensure that no American citizen can be turned away from a ballot box, regardless of his race or color..."

Banks sighed, and an involuntary smile blossomed on her face. She forgot, for a moment, the struggles of her own life and allowed herself to feel for the African American people of the nation, who were hopefully feeling some vindication, even amongst the ever-rocky terrain that was American society. The Civil Rights Act of 1964, and now the Voting Rights Act of 1965, were not nearly enough to make up for the atrocities committed on these people for centuries. Still, it is no disgrace to feel a victory, any victory, along the way. A sentiment that is often forgotten.

Even amongst this change, happening in front of her very eyes, Banks could not help wondering how fast progress was moving. Of course, she could not relate to the struggles of her colored neighbors, but even aside from that were moments in everyday life that always seemed to her as things that simply did not make sense. The most misogynistic and power-hungry of white men of the country, and to some extent the world, held society in a custom-tailored balance, theirs to control. How could one detail, such as a difference in skin pigment or difference in genitals, make them so blind to the ever-stretching worth of the human mind and soul? Such *humanity* that they toss to the side every day, for what? What could they possibly be so afraid of?

It's a founded fear, I suppose, Banks thought. *I know where Sergeant Nichols would be if I were in control. Then again, he wouldn't be there if he had treated me with respect in the first place.*

After spending some time thinking about this, Banks got up from her olive couch, washed her dishes, and got ready for bed, wondering all the time how she was going to spend the long hours of the weekend.

She used to have girlfriends, but they had all gone and done their own thing, marriage and kids, or sometimes doing the same as her, just as devoted and busy with their careers, just somewhere else. Isla banks had lived in Montgomery all her life, but she seemed to be one of the only people she knew who had stayed there. Not for any specific reason, just people traveling and drifting apart as they do.

Thinking about her fairly one-dimensional existence gave Banks a sinking feeling in her stomach. She remembered what the Sergeant had said in his office about chasing after something meaningless, and for a moment before regaining her senses, she wondered if that were true and if it was because she had little else to direct her attention.

But while the last of it may be true, Banks knew that it wasn't meaningless. At least one of Tom's murders had been self-defense, of that much Banks felt pretty certain. But 'pretty certain,' was not enough to convince anyone his sentence should be lessened (although any certainty at all from Banks seemed to prove useless anyway), not to mention the other victim still seemed to have been killed in cold blood. *And then* there was still the matter of the previous reputation from the affair, which Banks was *oh so excited* to hear about soon from Tom's own mouth.

Banks rolled her eyes at the thought. She thought for a moment about how she might berate Tom for that. She thought about how he would smile when she spoke to him, and she found herself smiling just thinking about it. She was then forced to recognize that, like earlier that day with Idgie, she was unintentionally considering

Tom Higgins an old friend or acquaintance rather than a piece of the puzzle. Tom should have been a routine work complication, not a routine catch-up, and Banks was a police detective, not a prison therapist.

As she closed her eyes to try and get some sleep, she wondered: *Am I getting too close to this?*

* * *

The sun is setting on the horizon. The ocean glitters in the afternoon light, peaceful and full of life. There is a boat floating out to sea, and she is in it. She does not row, but the vessel moves on its own, smoothly drifting, far away from any land. She does not know how she arrived here, but she admires the view around her, wondering where the boat is taking her.

As she drifts further and further out, the sunset becomes moonlight, and she becomes more anxious at the thought of being lost, as she does not even know what ocean she is in. Something in the water becomes visible, floating at the surface. The boat approaches it. As she comes closer, she can see a person working hard to keep their head above water. It is a young boy, and she is not sure where she has seen him before.

She comes even closer and attempts to call out to him, but he does not see her. He is looking down at the water just below his chin, panting as he keeps himself from drowning. He looks around frantically for help, but his eyes go past her boat, unable to see her there. She tries to call out again, but to no avail.

She is right next to him now and sees that he is looking down past the water, under it. She leans over the side of her boat to see what he is looking at, but can see nothing in the dark ocean. She sees how upset he is and decides that he needs help, and she is willing to provide it. He seems to have lost something beneath the water.

She hopes that the water is not too deep but takes a chance and dives over the side of the boat and into the murky depths. She is surprised to find that she is breathing fine underwater. Swimming ever lower, she searches for what could have been lost.

When she is so deep that she can no longer see the moonlight above, there is a soft green glow at the bottom. She thinks that this might be where the lost item is. Pushing onward, she eventually makes out the shape of a child in the dim glow. Seeing that the child is alone at the bottom of the ocean, she pushes even harder to reach them. The child wears a blue dress, her long hair hangs suspended in the water around her, and her complexion is pale and ghostly. The woman's view of the child is blurred through the water, but she can see that the child's eyes are closed, and her mouth hangs open, unconscious. This young girl seems to have been down here for a long time.

The protagonist reaches to grab the child's hand but comes up empty. One of the girl's arms is missing. She tries for the other hand, and the child opens her eyes. Her lifeless pupils stare at the woman, and not a moment later, the child chokes and shakes as she begins to drown. The woman panics and tries to collect the child, but she is suddenly pushed out of the way by a great white shark. She looks back at the child. There are two sharks there, and one bites on to the girl's empty sleeve and pulls her away into the darkness. The other shark looks at the woman, then disappears behind them.

The woman does not know why, but she knows the child's name. She calls out to her, staring into nothingness and screaming it...

* * *

MONDAY, AUGUST 9TH, 1965. 09:00 AM.

Monday morning, bright and early, Banks awoke and went into work. She had had a disturbing dream the night before, and she knew who it had been about.

"I realized that while I mighta been tryna keep floatin' all my life, she was sittin' at the bottom of the ocean with sharks hoverin' over her. And she didn't see the point of tryin' to get out because she was in too deep. She had never even seen the light of the sun. I never tried to make her feel like she was down there, but she already knew, just like always."

She tried not to dwell on the dream and focus on her objective, but she could not help but feel somewhat off even as she walked into the station.

She made no stops or pauses before marching straight to Sgt. Nichols' office. He looked up when she entered, sipping his coffee, and seemed genuinely surprised to see her.

"Banks," he said, setting his coffee down and folding his hands. He leaned back in his chair and looked up at her. "How can I help you?"

She did not falter; she felt no emotion. Her business was business itself. There was no room for roundabouts this morning.

"I need my badge, please," she said. "And my gun. The weekend's over, and I'm ready to work."

He looked disappointed at this request, but he obliged. He got Banks' things out of the drawer behind him and set them in front of her. "There you go, Detective. And this," he picked up a file folder that had been sitting on the desk as well and held it out to her as she picked up her badge, "this is the case you're workin' now."

Banks took the folder after securing both her gun and her badge. She knew that whatever it was, she would be happy when she saw it, so she decided she would open it once she was at her desk. It required a massive bit of effort to stand there in front of the Sergeant without saying something she shouldn't, and there was no use in assisting that urge.

"Thank you," she said. Not allowing another word, she turned and left. She was unsure if he had tried to say anything more because she had decided she wouldn't listen this morning.

When she reached her desk in the bullpen, she muttered a greeting to Wild, who was sitting at his desk that formed an angle with hers. He looked up from what he had been reading and gave her a look of surprise, as well.

"I wish everyone would stop looking at me like that this morning," she said, sitting down in her uncomfortable desk chair and setting the folder down in front of her, still reluctant to open it.

"Well," Wild said, quietly enough that Banks could tell he was trying to make a private comment, "When I heard you turned in your badge, I thought you'd up and left. Or been fired."

Banks snorted involuntarily. "Sarge wishes," she said. "Sent me on a long weekend to collect myself, or whatever. I think he thought I would give up and not come back."

Wild smiled a little. "He must not know you very well. I'm glad you didn't give up."

"Oh, he knows me plenty," Banks said. "That's the problem. He knows if he doesn't cut me down, I'll keep coming back to cause trouble like a weed."

She took a deep breath and finally opened the folder. The words 'missing person' and 'eighty-three years of age' caught her eye immediately.

"Oh, son of a bitch!" She exclaimed, feeling defeated and upset, precisely like she knew she would be.

"What?" Wild asked, somewhat startled by the exclamation this early in the morning.

"He's got me workin' that missing old lady case," she said, and she handed off the file for Wild to see. He looked at it for a moment and allowed himself a smirk.

"Wouldn't you know it?" He said. "You were right. Her husband was the one who reported her missing, he's listed with Alzheimer's, and from the picture, I'm pretty sure I've seen that woman down at the department store in Normandale."

"Loveman's," Banks said. "I know it. I'm pretty sure I've seen her there, too."

"She's probably home right now," Wild said, for once in his life looking like he might laugh, though he suppressed it. "Maybe you should just go check there."

"That is the last thing I feel like doing," she said, leaning on her desk and resting her head in her hands.

~ 11 ~

THE AFFAIR

Five days went by like molasses. By the time Banks' next visit with Tom Higgins came, she had solved the missing person case Sgt. Nichols had assigned her (get this: the woman had not even left the house. She was in the other room when he filed the report over the phone). There was also a vandalism case (spray paint in the same place every day that appeared around the same time, so it was only a matter of waiting for them to come by with their paint and arresting them. It ended up being some wannabe-hippie high school kid) and a whole lot of other nonsense. The Sergeant was purposefully giving Banks the bottom of the pile, so it felt even better to know that she was going against his direct orders now, even though it still made her panic a little bit if she thought about it too hard.

Saturday came, and Banks shot out of bed so quickly when her alarm went off that she felt a little lightheaded. The drive down to Dothan felt even longer that morning, as Banks was longing for something interesting to put a dent in the snooze fest that was her job at the moment.

She arrived and strolled confidently up to the office lady's desk, offering polite greeting but little else.

"You'll have an hour and a half," the woman said. "I arranged the solitary cell you usually use. I'm sure I don't need to remind you about the *cameras* in there, either, Detective?" She winked, and Banks felt an almost uncontrollable urge to roll her eyes.

"You sure do not," Banks said instead, smiling a little too hard to hide her discomfort. "Thank you."

The guard, who Banks now knew was named Ripley, showed her to the cell as he had done a good few times already. By this point, Banks was sure she could have found it herself, but she dared not say that because the office gossip there was already unnecessary. She didn't need Ripley and the office lady talking about how she wanted to escort *herself* to her *private* meeting with Mr. Higgins.

Once again, in a few short minutes, Banks found herself sitting across from a cheerful and handcuffed Tom Higgins, chipper as ever, who did not hesitate to take her silence as an invitation to begin himself.

"You seem a little quiet today, Detective," he said. "It's been a whole week, too. I was sure you'd got tired of me."

"Not quite, Tom," Banks said, managing a smile but feeling guilty. "It's been a long week, though."

Tom took this rare divulgence of personal feelings as an invitation to press further. "We could talk about *you* today if you wanted to," he said. "I still don't know your first name."

Banks looked up from opening her notepad and reciprocated his smile. "Oh no," she said. "I have fewer days with you now, and there's still so much to cover. Besides, we can't go getting too personal. The lady at the front desk and that guard already think I'm only here to get close to you."

You would have thought you had just told this prisoner he had been freed *and* somehow won the lottery, the way his face lit up.

"Detective Banks!" He exclaimed, feigning surprise. "What a damn scandal! You're better'n that, shame on you!"

Banks laughed with him, feeling like she had not done so in years.

* * *

Well, I hate to ruin our relationship, Detective, but I gotta feelin' you're gonna look at me a little differently when I tell you this portion of the story. Because this is perhaps the piece that I am most ashamed about.

Firstly, I'll tell you what the atmosphere is like around there, now, because it's all kinds of flipped around. By now, we was goin' into September, so we're gettin' down to the wire. The kids had been goin' to school, so Miss Diamond and the rest of 'em was gone most of the day, and when they came back, they had more work to do. So, I really didn't see Miss Diamond often. Every so often, she'd know when I was leavin' in the evenin', and she'd come out a second and say hello. We couldn't talk for long, though. Sure took the wind outta my sails.

But September also meant there was more harvestin' happening since it was in the season now, and that means us boys was all hands on deck in the trees, so there ain't much space to keep between us. Me and a couple of the other boys would talk and hang around the same area, just to keep company. Them boys kept me goin', that's for sure.

Oh, and I should tell ya, in case you were wonderin', Little Ricky Thomas died the last week in August that year of whatever he had. Poor kid. Some of us went over to his mamma's. We brought her some apples we stole from the orchard. Well, I say *stole*. I had asked Mrs. McMullen if we could take some to her, and she insisted that we did. She wanted to send somethin' over herself, but Mr. McMullen couldn't see the point, and what he said went, so they didn't.

Yeah, we was out there together, keepin' each other movin' along. It was hard to lose Ricky, but we had each other. The only one who didn't come by was exactly who you'd expect. Tuck's bruises had all but healed, but he still didn't say a thing to me or damn near anyone. He just let all that sit in him for so long. He hated my guts, I'll tell ya. He kept as far away from us as possible. I'd already tried to apologize to him on Miss Diamond's behalf, but he wouldn't hear it.

Well, I know you don't have a whole lot of time, so I'll just skip to the main of it: the first night I spent with Mrs. McMullen.

It was a Friday, September second. I was leavin' for the night. By now, I'm sure you've gotten the idea that I usually left last. Sun was goin' down. I was walkin' up to get on the road like always when Mrs. McMullen came out the back door, there. She was wavin' me down, so I figured she needed help with somethin'. I went up to the porch there and stood on the step. She asked me how I was doin', I said I was doin' fine, and then she asked me if I wanted to come inside.

I shoulda known somethin' was off when she asked me that because, as I've said before, I was not allowed in that house. None of us were. If they needed somethin' fixed in there, they had somebody else do it. Now, I *had* been in there, of course, just the one time when Miss Betty cut herself if you remember that, but Mr. and Mrs. McMullen didn't know about it.

Yeah, I shoulda known somethin' was goin' on, but I went in anyhow.

Even more interesting, she then asked me if I wanted some wine, and me just havin' turned eighteen, feelin' like an adult an' all, I took some. I didn't know this at the time, but she had already had a good bit. That's why she was talkin' so much. We was sittin' on the couch in the livin' room in there, and I was tryin' to be respectful, of course, but she sat down real close to me, and we were just talkin'.

"You know, Tom," she was saying, "you have always been so polite and caring, and I've always liked that about you."

I see you lookin' at me like that, Detective. I promise you, that *is* what she said.

I said, "Thank you, ma'am."

Then she said, "Oh, Tom, please. We've known each other for long enough; you can call me Violet."

Now I see you squirmin', Detective. I'm not as gullible as I seem. I knew somethin' was goin' on by this point. But you gotta understand, Mrs. McMullen was the last person I would expect somethin' like this from, so I let myself think that that couldn't be what was actually happenin'. She *is* a virtuous, Christian woman, after all.

Then we went on talkin, and I called her Violet 'cause she told me to. She was havin' more wine, and she kept pourin' me some, too. And I was drinkin' it, make no mistake, I had no problem doin' it. It was much better than drinkin' that cheap whiskey the boys'd find. And, not to make you uncomfortable, but I do remember thinkin' about how pretty she looked and how fuzzy I was feelin'.

After talkin' for a while, she said to me, "You know, Tom, my husband is out tonight. He's always out. Stays out drinkin' and doesn't come home 'til mornin'. And the kids went to my mother's house for the weekend this afternoon. Guess I invited you in here 'cause I was lonely. Ain't nobody here."

By this time, it was dark outside. "So, Mr. McMullen goes out a lot?" I asked her. "He never struck me as a party man."

She said, "He's not when he's here. He hardly does anything here at all. He pretends to do work in his office all day while you boys are runnin' the damn place, and then he goes out with his boys and does God knows what."

So I said, "Leaves you lonely a lot, I guess."

"Yeah," she said, and she sighed. "That's why I like havin' all them kids around. They give me somethin' to do sittin' around here all day."

So then I asked her if that's why they adopted Miss Diamond, and she said yes. Said she couldn't have any more kids of her own because the doctors tied her up after she had Billy, and she thought Mr. McMullen told 'em to do it because he didn't want any more. She also thought a kid with some kinda cripple like Miss Diamond had would occupy her even more. I told her I thought that was a nasty thing for them to do to her, and I think she liked that I said it.

"You know Tom," she said, "If it weren't for them kids, I wouldn't even stick around."

So I said, "He don't make you happy, do he?" And she said, "No."

Now, by then, it was pretty clear what was goin' on. Mrs. had been movin' closer to me on the couch, there, and I was lettin' her. I don't wanna tell you that it was the wine, because it wasn't just that, on either side. She was lonely and unhappy in her marriage, and I was there. Coulda been anyone, I guess.

Now, I'm ashamed to say that I had my own reasons for doin' what I did. I wasn't particularly happy at that point in my life, either. My buddy had just passed, I wasn't able to spend any time with my little friend, and Tuck's eyes were a needle in my back all the time. I'm not makin' excuses; make no mistake. The worst part of all of it was I thought about Miss Betty as her mamma was leadin' me upstairs. I wondered what she would think of me if she ever found out, but in my state, I decided I didn't care anymore.

After we'd done what we did, and the feelin' was wearin' off, I finally saw what had happened, and I sure felt like a real loser. I felt so guilty for doin' that, and so you'd wonder, "Tom, why did you do it again if you felt so bad?" Well, I don't know. I didn't know then, and I still don't. Mrs. McMullen was a lonely woman, and it felt like I was helpin' her. But all I ever did, in the end, was ruin everything.

"He *what?*" Tom responded to Banks, who sat in her chair holding back a smile after sharing the news with him. "Now, you're foolin' with me now, Detective, gotta be."

"I'm not, Tom," she said. "Johnnie Pritchett bought up the orchard with money his folks left him. Not only that, he's married to Idgie McMullen, now."

"*No shit!*" He said, astonished. "Little Idgie? That old dog, I'll tell ya. Well, I guess she'll be a whole lady now, huh?"

Banks had brought up her visit to the orchard to cheer Tom up because he looked like he was ready to break down and cry after talking about the affair with Violet McMullen. He had come out of his story and hung his head, and Banks felt the immediate need to introduce remedy, making it all the more clear that she was in a new zone of familiarity with her suspect. At that moment, however, she decided that she was allowed to show compassion. If the Sergeant knew she was thinking that, she would be discharged immediately, whether or not she was even allowed to be there in the first place.

Fuck him, she thought.

It had made Banks all the more frustrated seeing Tom that way because it reaffirmed her suspicions that Tom Higgins was not a bad man, regardless of his crimes. This was a new complexity that Banks had not yet experienced in her short time as a detective. Most of the time, people who were guilty of crimes like murder were generally wicked, in one way or another. Banks could almost always discern the ruffians from the falsely accused. Never before had it been so gray, and such complexity to be coming from a self-proclaimed, "simple man."

As Tom sat there across from her, Banks was reminded of how rough he had looked when she met him for the first time. It had only been about three weeks before, but Tom had been looking more and more like the young man he still was underneath the prisoner facade. Now, his hair and beard had been cut back some, and life was slowly returning to his twinkling eyes. This was not the result of physical health. The prison had not just recently decided to focus on inmate health, which, honestly, they rarely did before. No, this change in Tom Higgins' face resulted from emotional healing, benefits driven from regular contact that bothered to ask about the man or anything at all. A friendly conversation does wonders for a broken soul.

Banks wondered if she should tell him about his father's collection or that she had gone to his house at all. After all, she was not meant to be solving a case, a detail that she often struggled to remember. Could Tom tell that this was something different? Or was he just glad for the company and therefore felt no need to question her intentions?

As Tom continued his story, Banks found herself writing less as she watched him slowly crawl back out of the darkness, back into the life he once had.

Well, that was that. It got real interestin' when Miss Diamond found out. Oh, yeah, she knew about it. Don't think me crude, Detective. I didn't discuss the details with her or anything like that. I wouldn't've told her at all, but she caught me comin' out of Mrs. McMullen's room one night a little later that week. I thought I was gonna melt into the floor when she saw me. I told her I couldn't talk then, but I'd be around on Saturday, and we would talk about it then.

So Saturday came, and Miss Diamond was up there on the back porch waitin' for me when I got there first thing in the mornin'. She came out to the trees with us, and I was wantin' to talk to her about it in private because nobody knew about it, but she decided she was gonna ask me with Johnnie and Jimmy and a couple other boys around.

We'd started workin', and she just went ahead and asked me, "So what were you doin' comin' outta their bedroom the other night?"

Johnnie and them looked up at me, and when they saw how red my face got, they stopped what they were doin' and waited for me to answer.

I said, "Miss Diamond, can we talk about this when the boys ain't here?"

She said, "Why, was it somethin' bad you were doin' in there with Mrs.?"

I remember it like it was yesterday, the looks on those boys' faces. Jimmy had these big wide eyes like he was caught in head-lights, and Kitch just started laughin' right away, with his hand over his mouth like he was tryin' to hold it back, but he knew damn well he wasn't. Johnnie was shocked, but he was smilin' too. After a while, he started laughin' too.

Miss Diamond smiled at them but was still a little confused. She wasn't ignorant, but I can't imagine she'd had much experience hearin' about stuff like that. She probably wouldn't have expected that from me, either.

"Miss Diamond," I said, smilin' a little from bein' embarrassed but tryin' to be a little serious, "you can't go tellin' nobody else about you seein' me, understand? Mr. McMullen finds out he'll have me hangin' from the flag pole, you'd better believe it."

"So, you *was* doin' somethin' wrong," she said. "You're gettin' with Mrs."

The boys could barely control themselves. Understand, bein' in the hot sun all day long does a lot to your brain, 'til you can barely hold it together anymore. They were glad for the entertainment, I'm sure. When Miss Diamond said that, they stopped for a moment to look at me, waitin' to hear it from the man himself.

I said, "Guess I am, but I ain't gonna do it no more."

Miss Diamond didn't seem like she cared if I was doin' it or not; she was just curious. The others were full of questions, some I wouldn't repeat to you or anyone, buncha hooligans. They did ask me why, though, besides what *they* were thinkin' was the reason, of course. After I made 'em swear not to tell no one, I told them about the McMullens' marriage, how Mr. McMullen didn't really care that much about anyone but himself and his drinkin' buddies. And also how Mrs. McMullen wanted babies around to keep her busy and give her a purpose, and how Mr. McMullen had the doctors tie her up, and that's how Miss Diamond ended up there in the first place.

Miss Diamond didn't get upset or ask too many questions, she just stayed and listened as we were workin', and when I was done sayin' my piece, she finally put her thoughts in.

"That son of a bitch," she said. We was all a little surprised because she ain't never swore before, and I wasn't sure if I should let her or not, but I figured she was with friends, so it was alright.

She said, "Why does he get to do that to her? He never does anything but get mad and leave."

Us boys were just raisin' eyebrows and sayin' nothin'. We all looked at each other, wonderin' if we should say anything, 'cause it usually wasn't our place to say anythin' bad about anyone around the family. But Miss Diamond was a little more than just part of the family.

"Well, Miss Diamond," I said, "You know he does what he can. I'm sure it ain't really that bad. And don't you go thinkin' of doin' nothin' about it, neither, or gettin' any of these boys involved, either."

They all laughed at that, and I made Miss Diamond promise me she wouldn't go tryin' anything like she did with Tuck. She agreed though she didn't look like she was ready to be done with it. We stopped there, and she stayed with us until they called her back for lunch.

Ol' Johnnie Pritchett, huh? Ain't that somethin'. It's funny that I'm rememberin' him as a farmhand, and he's runnin' it now. Wonder how he's doin..."

09:25 AM.

As Tom paused to reminisce, Banks chose then to interject since she figured they didn't have too much time left to talk.

"So, Diamond didn't like him, either," she said.

Tom looked at her again, this time with some fog lingering in his eyes.

"No," he said, blinking a little and bringing himself back from memory lane. "Nobody did, really. But he was the boss, and we had respect for him. No, he wasn't the friendliest of people, if he spoke to ya at all. But he wasn't as bad as he seemed. Sometimes a person can be the nicest you've met, doesn't mean anyone who marries them is happy."

Banks recognized this to be true, of course, and made a mental note of how Tom had changed the subject. She was not sure if this was his typical rambling or if it was intentional misdirection.

"You saw her again, though, didn't you?" Banks asked. "Even though you said you weren't going to. You were there the night of the twenty-first."

Tom let his face go slack and sighed. "Yeah," he said. "I saw her a few times more. *That* one was for a good reason, though."

"What was the reason?" Banks asked, any exhaustion that lingered from the week shedding immediately at the topic of the scene of the crime.

"Well," Tom said, a little hesitant, "that day, when Miss Diamond was out there with us, later on when I was leavin', she met me outside and told me she was wantin' to run away."

Banks waited patiently for a puzzle piece to slot into place as Tom was speaking. This felt crucial now. This was where things changed.

"She asked me if I wanted to come with her," he continued. "She figured I was her only friend in the world and the only person she wanted to come along. I tried to tell her she could stay behind and have a good life, but she wouldn't budge. She knew she didn't want to be there anymore, especially now that she knew she'd only been in the picture as somethin' to keep Mrs. McMullen occupied."

"And...?" Banks asked. "What did you say?"

Tom smiled a little at her fascinated persistence. "I said I'd go. There was no real reason I had to stay, although I'd miss those boys and, as much as I hated to admit it, I'd miss seein' Betty, too. But I knew it was probably for the best for me if I left, plus then Miss Diamond wouldn't be all alone."

"But you never got to go," Banks said, feeling an involuntary drop in her chest, a sudden sadness that she was not expecting to feel.

Tom looked down. "No," he said, "No, I didn't."

~ 12 ~

STILL IN THE WOODS

* * *

The orchard was alive and glowing in the Alabama sunshine. A regular day's work was being done. Birds were singing, and there was a distant sound of children laughing.

She walked through the rows of apple trees, looking up at the green leaves and bright yellow apples, blinking in the light of the sun. She shifted her gaze to look down the row, and a boy was walking toward her. He wore a t-shirt and overalls and old brown shoes that looked like they were closer to falling apart with every step. He was tanned from working in the sun, and his skin glowed from the sweat. His dark hair was short to allow him as much air as possible, and even when he was many feet away from her, she could see his blue eyes twinkling like the ocean would be at that moment, somewhere far away.

As he came closer to her, she felt a soothing calmness flow over her, like she was blanketed in a cloud, holding her up, so she felt no effort in standing or walking. She waited for him to come ever nearer and watched him smile when he stood close to her. His smile enveloped her being and convinced her that everything was going to be okay. The world and all its inconveniences fell away until they were left, just the two of them.

She looked up into his eyes and thought she could dive right in...

* * *

SUNDAY, AUGUST 15, 03:26 AM.

Isla Banks woke up in her bed, still laying as she had been, facing up at the ceiling, with her eyes shot wide open. It was still dark, and she did not have to be awake for at least another three hours or so. She took a moment to take in as much of her surroundings as she could without her glasses. Then she tried to reevaluate what she had just seen in her dream.

That boy was Tom Higgins, as he had looked in 1955, the picture of youth and happiness. Banks had only seen *that* Tom in his mugshot, but there was no denying that it had been him. The dream had not held even a glimpse into the malicious future event that would turn his world upside down and forever change him in the eyes of the world and the people he cared about the most.

It wasn't so much how he seemed to be feeling that occupied Banks' mind as she tried in vain to go back to sleep. What threw her about the dream was how *she* was feeling and felt still. Tom was not only an innocent young man in the dream, but he was also... lovable? The way he had looked into her eyes, and they had stood there in that moment, implying continuation. It was all the more frustrating, given his history, but it was almost like Banks was willing to put it aside, just to be there, with *him*...

It can't be, she thought.

MONDAY, AUGUST 16, 1965. 09:00 AM.

Monday came, and from the moment she woke up, all the way into the station, Banks found herself entangled in considerations and imaginings about Tom and his story. She wished it was just his *story* that she found herself thinking about, if for no other reason than wanting Ripley and the office lady to be proven wrong. That was strangely the thing that Banks thought most about when considering her feelings.

Besides that, she was excited for the story to continue as it grew ever nearer to the resolution. She wondered if there was more to the story as she had initially hoped there would be, so long as Tom would be honest. He already seemed to be franker with her than he had ever been with detectives in the past. For one thing, he wouldn't have told any of them about the McMullens' unhappy marriage in relation to the affair, not in detail anyway. Banks was certain he likely told her because she was a woman, but she decided to consider it an advantage rather than a nuisance for the sake of her pride.

Banks had also never seen anything about Tom's intention to run away with Diamond, and from the way he had been slow to mention it, Banks was sure he had not told many others before, if he told anyone. The thought of the two of them running away together made her heart hurt, and she wondered where they would be if they had managed it. How happy would the two of them be now?

Then, Banks thought: *where is Diamond now?*

Was she even alive? Banks had not explored the possibility of Tom killing her since the beginning because she struggled to convince herself it was possible.

If he didn't, Banks thought, *then Diamond is still out there somewhere. Assuming she took the gun, did she get much further than Louisiana? How long ago was she there? She could have been in California for years now, or maybe she looped around and ended up in Michigan or Ohio. Perhaps she even left the country. She'd be twenty-three now, and she spent pretty much her whole childhood running and hiding. Did she ever finally find somewhere to stay, or is she still running, even to this day? What kind of life has she known these past ten years?*

Banks knew there was a genuine possibility that she would never know the answer to these questions.

In the station, Banks sat down at her desk next to Wild, who sipped coffee like he always did, nodding when he saw her arrive.

When she had settled in, Wild started a conversation with her, a rarity so few it startled her.

"We have a new case together," he said, low and monotonous. "It's mine, of course, but it's a good case. Robbery downtown. Much more interesting than a missing old lady."

Banks could see that Wild was, in his way, making a real effort to cheer her up. Poor thing, too. She had left him last with a bit of a fright last time she saw him.

The previous Friday, Banks had had a complete meltdown in the station after the Sergeant left for the day (early, for no good reason), yelling about how unreasonable he was. The other officers let her go until Detective Jefferson came over and gave her a side hug, attempting to relieve her stress by telling her a story about the lousy bagel she'd had that morning.

A specific conversation had been the primary inspiration for the meltdown. The Sergeant had come out and leaned on the edge of Banks' desk as he notified her of several jobs he knew in offices going and that it might suit her to find something that did not stress her out so much.

"I'm fine, Sarge," she had said, teeth gritted in a false smile as she looked up at him from her desk chair. "I like my job."

"Well, just be careful, now," Sgt. Nichols had responded, looking around at the other detectives, who were trying to look like they were not listening. "Watch these boys in here, pretty thing like yourself. You never know what they might want from you."

Banks glanced around and saw that not one person was looking in their direction, but it was almost silent even as they tried to look busy, looking at anything but the two of them. Wild was staring with intensity at the papers on his desk, idle pen in hand as he sat, motionless.

"These are good men, Sarge," Banks said. "I'm not worried about them."

"Ain't no such thing as a good man, doll," the Sergeant said in a low tone, turning his head down to look her in the eye, and then a little further south while he was at it. "You got energy, fellas like that. If I were you, I'd keep a lookout."

It might have been a decent piece of advice if it weren't for the look in his eye as he looked her up and down. She had seen that act before in crime files: the altruistic professional man with not even enough respect for his victim to go as far as consider his motives, 'ulterior.' This was not advice. It was a warning, a threat.

"Believe me, Sarge," she said, every trace of a smile dropped from her expression. "I won't let anyone get the better of me."

Even the other officers at the station could see how Nichols treated Banks, not that they would stand up and say anything, of course. Jefferson was the only other woman in the station, and she seemed pretty resigned to the life of a female officer and had no problem taking easy cases that didn't take a lot of time. She was older, her children grown and gone, so she didn't feel the need to overexert like Banks did. But she tried her best to be kind, and if anyone asked her for anything, she did everything she could to help. Regardless of their difference in style, Banks respected Jefferson for that reason.

During that episode, Banks remembered how deeply uncomfortable Wild had looked, sitting at his desk pretending to read something. At the time, the last thing she was thinking about was making a man more comfortable with her valid feelings. Still, in retrospect, she did feel a little bad for causing an upset and hoped she wouldn't suffer for this unusual blip in her professionalism.

Banks smiled at Wild. "That's good," she said. "It'll be nice to work a case together again."

Wild let out the breath he had been holding onto and nodded. This was Wild's way of saying, *I'm relieved you're not going nuts again, and I'm also glad about this case.*

10:03 AM.

Wild and Banks were sitting in Wild's Impala, getting ready to head downtown to the corner store that suffered a robbery. The past few weeks put Banks all out of whack, and both detectives were grateful for a return to routine.

Banks sat with a little more tension than Wild, though, because she was considering whether or not she should tell Wild about her unauthorized side work with the Higgins case (she certainly wouldn't tell him about the recent emotional developments in her involvement). She was not sure how he would react to her disobedience of direct orders. While she was exploring this dilemma, Wild began a conversation of his own.

"I closed the Haroldson case," he said.

"Oh, yeah!" Banks said, recalling the subject. "I forgot to ask you about it. Can I ask how it went?"

Wild's pause before speaking made Banks' heart sink a little. She hoped he wasn't going to say what she thought he might. Fortunately, he looked over at her and radiated contentment that could only mean good news.

"The kid's gonna walk," he said.

Banks smiled back at him. "What turned it around?"

"Well," Wild said, looking as proud as his features could manage, "I convinced the judge to allow a search warrant, under the grounds that the victim's wife was acting suspiciously and kept changing her story every time we asked her anything. I was certain we would find something if we went to the house."

"And?" Banks asked, visibly excited enough for the both of them.

"And we found his suicide note in the nightstand. Not his, *hers.* He'd left it behind, tellin' his wife he was gonna off himself and where he was gonna do it. Fingerprints and the signature on it match up. Victim's old lady hid it from us on purpose, and even when we found it, she still refused to confess. Wasn't 'til we told her we could get her a fine, and she wouldn't have to go to prison for it, even though I thought she should have, that she admitted to hidin' it. Said it was too painful for the family to know he killed himself, and I'm sure it is, but that's no excuse to condemn some innocent colored boy, just 'cause he saw it happen."

"Wow," Banks said, still smiling. "Well, you were right, Wild. You knew it didn't feel right, and you exposed the truth."

"Yeah," he said. "Felt pretty good. So how have you been?"

Wild pressed the brake and put the car in reverse, slowly beginning to pull out of the parking spot. Banks gave her response almost no rational thought.

"I've been working the Higgins case," she blurted out. "Against Sarge's orders. But you can't tell anyone."

Wild pushed the brake and put the car back into park. He looked at her and raised his eyebrows slightly, which for Wild meant that he was filled to the brim with shock. "Banks," he said, definitely surprised but with almost no change in tone, "You could get in a load of trouble for that."

"I know," she said, keeping a calm tone herself while praying on the inside that he wouldn't tell the Sarge on her. "I know, Wild. But I'm in too deep, now. I can't stop until I'm at the end of it."

Wild looked forward again and resumed pulling out of the spot. He let a second pass as he pulled out of the lot and onto the road, immediately finding traffic. When they were stopped in said traffic, he looked over at her again.

"Can't say I understand," he said. "I mean, I don't know if I believe that case is worth losin' your job over. But," Wild took a breath to collect his thoughts before continuing, "I suppose only you know how you're feeling about it. We gotta trust our gut. Another officer might've figured that Haroldson case was open and shut, and that innocent boy woulda been jailed or hanged for no good reason."

Banks nodded as Wild slowly continued driving, patiently moving along with the flow of traffic. When he looked at her again, he nudged her shoulder with his fist and managed the smallest of grins.

"Do what you gotta do, Detective," he said. "That's what the Sarge tells me to do, and I figure he may never say that to you, so I'll be the one to."

Banks thought she might cry right then, mostly because she was exhausted. But she sincerely appreciated how cool Wild was about this. She was glad they were on an assignment together again.

05:41 PM.

Banks and Wild were once again sitting at their desks in the bullpen. Many of the others had already left for the day, including Sgt. Nichols. They trucked along on working the robbery case, but Wild also took the opportunity to inquire about Banks' findings in her off-the-record work while they took a break to eat their respective packed dinners.

"I'm almost certain at least one was self-defense," Banks was telling him, gesturing as she spoke with a potato chip. "I was right to begin with: Tom Higgins is not a killer, not on purpose anyway. No one would have the kindness and respect he has if they planned a killing like that or even did it in cold blood in the moment. I can't find anything that would have suggested to that attorney that Tom had premeditated."

"That's pretty serious," Wild said, picking at a chicken breast with a fork. "He wouldn't be sitting on a thirty-year sentence for self-defense. A few years, maybe, but not *thirty*. No chance." Wild shoveled a big bite down and only chewed a little before continuing. "What about your dead girl theory?"

"I was never all that convinced by it," she responded, rolling her eyes and smiling at Wild talking with his mouth full. "Even less so now. At this point, I'd be shocked if that were true. Jesus, Wild? Was that a *softball* you just put in your mouth?"

Banks laughed, and Wild looked like he was on the verge of doing the same through his effortful chicken-chewing. Once he got his food down successfully, Wild continued.

"So you're pretty sure it was self-defense," he said. "Have you gotten any evidence that supports that?"

"Not yet," Banks said, begrudgingly. "Just a few opinions. No eyewitness accounts and no other evidence. Tom himself hasn't even said it, but I noticed that he neither confirmed nor denied the theories of the prosecuting attorney. He said that he killed them, but the story the attorney came up with seems to be entirely his. But why Tom would have allowed it if it weren't true, now, that's something I'm still confused about."

"Hmm," Wild pondered. "Well, he must have a reason why he let it go in the first place if you're right. And whatever the reason is, he seems to be sticking to it. If only you had someone, you could ask who was there, but no other witnesses attested to seeing the act itself."

Convenient Diamond McMullen isn't here, Banks thought. She was becoming more and more convinced that Diamond had been there and seen something before running.

"Wild, what do you think about the runaway?" She asked, having wholly neglected her dinner for thinking too hard to do anything else.

Wild had not neglected his and was still chewing when he began his following sentence. "She must have seen something important," he said. "Maybe she ran so they couldn't get anything out of her."

"That's what I was thinking," Banks said. "Although, Tom did say she wasn't a big talker, and she probably wouldn't have given him away anyway. Maybe he convinced her to go anyway since he knew she wanted to run anyway."

"Could be." It then seemed to occur to Wild that it might be rude for him to eat when his companion wasn't, so he took one more bit and closed the Tupperware container his wife had packed for him and sat back in his chair. "Or maybe she just ran. Maybe she didn't see anything."

"Not if she took that gun," Banks reminded him. Wild looked disappointed in himself for having forgotten. In his defense, he had not been as neck-deep in this case as Banks had. "No, it seems more likely she was there, saw Tom kill the two men, took the gun, and ran away to keep her knowledge and the murder weapon away from the authorities. Even if it was self-defense, Diamond McMullen likely never had much faith in any authority. I'm certain she didn't. She probably figured she was doing him a favor, whether he asked her to or not."

"Mmhm," Wild agreed. "Seems likely to me. But it's not enough to have a solid theory without evidence, especially since you'll have to convince the higher-ups it's even a worthy endeavor since they already pulled it. No, you're gonna need something irrefutable to win 'em over."

Banks knew he was right. One tipping point in the story could lead to the dominos falling, leading her to the resolution that confirmed her theory. But she had not come across anything like that, and she wasn't sure how much longer she would be able to keep this up before being caught.

Just then, something seemed to occur to Wild. "You know," he said, "even though there are no eyewitnesses to the crime that we know of, something that always helps me is talking to someone who was close by. Especially someone who knew the killer well."

Banks felt like she had finally woken up from a long sleep at this consideration and immediately felt foolish not to have thought of that before. "You're absolutely right, Wild. And I even know what city to look in."

~ 13 ~

ELIZABETH MILLER

It took almost no time to find her. Idgie Pritchett had already mentioned to Banks that her sister, Betty, lived in Enterprise, now, and given Banks a married name. So Banks barely needed to do more than open an Enterprise phone book to find Mrs. Elizabeth Miller, wife of Ronald Miller and mother of two.

Banks' Bel-Air was already driving through the streets of Enterprise, Alabama, at eight o'clock Tuesday morning, and she was all the while feeling grateful that Wild was looking after her back home. Now that he knew about her secret investigation, he promised to cover for her absence by telling the Sergeant she was working the robbery case with him. So while he was out in Montgomery tracking leads, she was over in Dale county, parking on the street in front of a suburban single-family home, 4073 Franklin Street.

Banks got out of her car and looked at the house. It was a pastel yellow color, with brown trim and front door, and some brick detailing that was so neat, it looked like it was laid just a day earlier. There was a burgundy Ford Mustang in the driveway, sparkling clean from the paint to the chrome wheels, shining in the morning sun. The yard was neatly kept and evenly green, but there was no sight of any flower garden or garden at all. Banks thought the property looked like it was ready to be sold or photographed for an advertisement. The whole scene was, Banks thought, lacking a little character. It was a different perfect than the farmhouse on the orchard, with its flower gardens and rustic charm. The only uniqueness this house possessed was a single apple tree in the front yard.

Banks took a breath and started to walk up the drive, up the three porch steps, and to the front door, which showed no sign of scuff or dirt. Banks wondered for a moment if she had the wrong house, even with the numbers proclaiming "4073" above the door knocker, all of which were polished brass. Banks had just gotten in front of it, raising her hand to knock. Before she could make contact, the door opened, revealing a man who looked to be in his early thirties, dressed in a gray business suit and fedora hat, carrying a brown leather briefcase that perfectly matched the shade of his brown loafers. As young as he was, Banks could not help but think his fashion sense was outdated by a decade or two. It was a *little* different, she thought, in comparison to her white, short-sleeved button-down tucked into her high-waisted houndstooth pants, her cat-eye glasses, and black and white oxfords. She would not have expected anyone to go out wearing a full suit and hat these days, especially in August in Alabama.

When the man caught sight of Banks standing there, he flinched from shock, staring with wide eyes through his silver wire-frame glasses. When his surprise passed, he put a hand to his chest and smiled, laughing a little at his startled reaction. Banks returned the smile politely, allowing him to speak first.

"Oh, my," he said, "I'm sorry. I was just leaving for work, and I wasn't expecting anyone to be standing there."

"Of course," Banks responded, removing her badge from her pocket and showing it to him. "My name is Isla Banks. I'm a detective from over in Montgomery."

Oh no, she thought, *what happened to the backstory from last time?* No one ever wanted Banks working undercover for some reason, so she was so used to being herself when investigating, she was not used to keeping to a story, even one so close to her real-life as this. She tried to recover herself to offer some continuity, lest Idgie would talk to her sister and realize their stories didn't match up.

"Well, detective-in-training," she corrected herself, hoping he wouldn't wonder about her fully qualified police badge. "We're researching old cases to be tested on procedure and collection of evidence, all that jazz. I was wondering: is there an Elizabeth Miller here perchance?"

The man seemed somewhat skeptical, as most often would be when there was police on their doorstep, but he seemed to accept her intentions. Banks was unsure whether it was because he thought it was expected or if he would be late to work soon and did not have the time to ponder the situation. Either way, he obliged her request.

"Yes," he said, "that's my wife. I'm Ron Miller. Nice to meet you." He put his hand out and gave her a firm handshake, then he turned back into the house and called, "Eliza!"

Bank was mildly concerned that he called her that, and thought that there was a real chance she had found the wrong Elizabeth Miller. She bit her lip as they waited for the lady of the house, but when she finally came into view, Banks was immediately reassured.

Eliza Miller, once called Betty McMullen, appeared next to her husband in a deep blue, knee-length shift dress, a startling sight of modernity compared to her husband's fashion. Her red hair was up in a ponytail, and she had the slightest touch of tasteful makeup on her face, through which her natural freckles were still somewhat visible, though they were not as pronounced as her sister Idgie's had been. She looked from her husband to Banks, and when she spoke, her melodic voice put a cooling feeling in Banks' ears.

"Hello," she said to Banks, who again felt like she was meeting a character out of a storybook. "How can I help you?"

Ron Miller intercepted a quick apology, assuring them he would love to stay, but he needed to get to work. He kissed his wife and nodded to Banks, who nodded back. When he was in the driver's seat of the burgundy Mustang and pulling out of the drive, Banks answered the question hanging in the air. This time, she chose to be honest.

"My name is Detective Isla Banks," she said. "I'm here to ask you about what happened ten years ago at your family's orchard."

08:25 AM.

Eliza Miller had reacted with perfect grace, never faltering or showing any air of panic. She had simply nodded and let Banks inside as though Mrs. Miller had been expecting her visit. They were alone in the house, as the children would have been on their way to school already. It was spookily quiet, and Banks wondered how it sounded when everyone was home.

Eliza showed the detective to the front sitting room, which, like the outside of the house, lacked pizzaz. The furniture was placed parallel and perpendicular in straight lines and perfect angles, there was no speck of dust on any of the deep walnut furniture, and the beige carpet looked as though it had never been walked on. There were no knick-knacks on any surfaces, but a few pictures were sparingly placed on the cream-colored walls, one of which was a large photograph of the McMullen farmhouse, viewed from the side with the beginning of the trees peeking into the image. When Eliza sat down on an armchair, positioned a perfect right angle from the sofa where Banks sat, she noticed that the shade of blue on both pieces of furniture matched Eliza's dress perfectly. Banks knew her own home was exceedingly neat as well, and she liked it that way, but at least her home looked like someone was living there.

Banks was not sure how to start the conversation, as Eliza Miller waited for her to begin, looking friendly but undeniably concerned while doing so. Banks decided a polite and complimentary opener would be sufficient to start.

"You have a lovely home," she said. "You must work yourself to the bone to keep it *this* clean with two children."

Eliza smiled at her. She was still apprehensive, but Banks could tell the comment was much appreciated. "Oh, I sure do," she said. "Takes a shrewd eye and a lot of effort, but Ron likes a neat house, too, so he does his share."

Not surprising, Banks thought.

"Good," she said. "If you don't mind my asking, what inspired the change from 'Betty' to 'Eliza'?"

Eliza remained with a smile, but there was visible sadness present in her eyes. Banks made a mental note to be careful when asking about Eliza's past. It was clear from her behavior, as well as what Banks learned from Idgie, that the woman sitting in front of her was an entirely different person than the young girl she once was, the one that lived in Tom Higgins' mind. Nevertheless, she answered Banks' question.

"If I'm honest," she said, "I needed a change of life. When, well... when *it* happened, I had a real hard time bringing myself back from it."

"And that's why you moved away, too?" Banks asked, keeping her tone even and quiet so as not to spook the woman.

Eliza sighed and stared at the wall just past Banks with a blurred focus. "I couldn't stop thinkin' about what happened. Every time I walked past the barn or did anything at all, I just found myself thinking about it again. And Mamma was no help. She wouldn't tell us anything about what happened or any of the other stuff. She still never talks about it."

Banks was beginning to understand Eliza's change in behavior in her life. After something so traumatic happening, being offered no explanation or counsel turns a bad situation worse. She had not been given the tools to work through what happened to her father, and thus gone from a happy young girl with a bright future to a shadow of herself. She still managed to have a good life, but she had nothing that made her feel enough joy to display in her house or fill any of the time she now spent cleaning and raising her children.

She was likely using her children to occupy her unhappy existence, just like her mother had done.

"I'm sorry to be bringing this up for you again," Banks said.

Eliza brought her focus back to her guest, looking a little confused. "Oh no," she said. "I'm almost relieved to talk about it. No one would tell me anything. I had to search for my own answers. You probably know everything about it, but Mamma kept me far away from the whole thing because she thought it would upset me. What *really* upset me was being told that the boy I had loved killed my father and not even being allowed to speak to him or ask him why."

Banks felt a dagger in her heart listening to Eliza speak about Tom. *What is it about this man,* she thought, *that makes people love him so much that the sadness that follows swallows them up and spits them back out, hollow and broken? If my hunch is wrong, and he killed those men in cold blood, then turned around and lied to me and everyone else... Well, if that's true, this man is the Devil himself. Even still, I can't convince myself that it is.*

"Well," Banks said, "if it's alright, then. I can start with what I wanted to talk to you about. You see, I've been visiting Tom Higgins in prison—"

"You've seen him?" Eliza interrupted, and a flash of light shone through her eyes for the briefest of moments, and Banks caught a glimpse of young Betty peeking through the surface.

"Yes, I have," Banks responded, almost smiling but still tiptoeing.

Eliza let out a breath and did not change her expression. "How is he?" she asked.

Banks was interested, though not particularly surprised with Eliza's immediate curiosity about Tom's wellbeing. She was undoubtedly kind and had probably never known how she should feel about him after what he did.

"He's fine," Banks said. "A little longing for company, he's always overjoyed when I go to talk to him." She took a risk with her following statement. "He talks about you all the time."

Banks held her breath, waiting for Eliza's reaction, and her regrettably over-empathetic heart broke when a single tear fell down Eliza's cheek. Banks went to stammer an apology but decided it might be better to steer in the direction they were going, all the while attempting not to upset her further.

"I know he did wrong," Banks said, "but it wasn't because he never cared, Eliza. He cared a lot, still does. I don't know why he did what he did, but I can't imagine his heart has changed too much from when you knew him."

Another tear fell from Eliza's cheek, but her expression was not that of upset. Instead, she listened to Banks speak with hopeful eyes, breathing shakily. When Banks finished speaking the last time, Eliza surprised her by smiling and even letting out a soft chuckle. She looked relieved.

"Oh my," she said, wiping the tears from her face. "Gosh, I didn't know I needed to hear that." She took another moment to collect herself, seeming a little embarrassed by her loss of composure while maintaining the smile of relief she wore. "I really am a mess over this, aren't I?"

Banks smiled at her and tried to reassure her. "Eliza, this was not something that happens every day. I'd be concerned if you weren't."

Eliza nodded in agreement. "If I can ask: why are you asking about this, now? That was ten years ago. I'm grateful to talk to someone about this, but surely you didn't come here to be a therapist."

Again, Banks decided that pure honesty was ideal for dealing with someone who had good intentions but was still so fragile. It would do Eliza no good to be fooled and manipulated when she had been through all that already.

"No," Banks answered. "Eliza, Tom's case was reopened. They found the gun he used over in Louisiana, and they brought it back. It had two sets of fingerprints on it, so it was just enough to warrant a reopening. I have a personal interest in this case, just curiosity, really. I would usually have a partner with me, but my acting Sergeant pulled the case because they were concerned whether it was worth it, so I've been looking into it as a side project."

Now who's the therapist? Banks thought. She scolded herself for being too open, but she stood by her decision, to be honest. And it was well-received. Eliza listened intently as Banks spoke, sincere and polite.

"I see," Eliza said. "So, do you think he was falsely charged?"

Banks wished she had a definite answer but searched within herself for her true thoughts and carefully managed to put them into coherent words. "I think there is more to the story than it seems. I think there's a chance it could have either mostly or completely self-defense, which would be punished still, but not for as long as Tom is sentenced. I'm not sure about total innocence, but there's something he isn't telling me, and I don't know why. Because if he is serving too long, why wouldn't he want to save himself?"

Eliza shifted from ponderance to complete understanding. "Tom was always a virtuous boy. Real honest, but he'd put anyone before himself. That's what confused me about it all. If you'd have asked me before it happened, I'd have said he'd have let himself die before hurtin' someone else. And the affair, too? Now that one threw me for a loop so bad, I could hardly be upset about it. Nobody properly told me about that part of it until a decent while after, though I pretty much knew. Us kids weren't allowed in the trial, none of us, and Mamma kept our ears clean of it. S'pose she didn't want us to think badly of her. I'd probably do the same."

Banks was thankful for Eliza's increasing comfort in the situation. Carefully taking this opportunity, Banks decided to begin questioning her properly.

"Can I ask you to tell me about that night?" Banks asked. "From your perspective. I know you probably didn't see any of it, but you must have heard the shots at least?"

Luckily, Eliza kept the pace with Banks, moving along in the story without dwelling on the emotion of it for too long. While

Banks wanted Eliza to be able to feel what she had likely been suppressing for so long, she also wanted to get somewhere with the story. She also did not take the whole day to do so. Wild was back in Montgomery covering for her, and she did not want to inconvenience him longer than necessary. In ordinance with Banks' method, Eliza gave what she could.

"Well, the day hadn't been anything unusual," she said. "It was a Wednesday; we had all been in school earlier. I'd been taking care of the kids with Mamma all afternoon while they did their homework. Mamma never acted strangely in the time she and Tom would have been doin' what they were doin', so I never suspected anything. And Diamond, oh, that sweet child. When I look back, she was bein' a little extra talkative that day. She was always so quiet. I didn't know it at the time, but she was plannin' on runnin' away that night. She was tellin' the girls to leave her alone and pushin' 'em back even when Mamma told 'em all to stop. I s'pose Diamond wanted to say what was on her mind before she left. I knew she didn't like the others all that much, but I didn't realize she was so unhappy all the time. Poor thing, she could never find any contentment there, except when she was with Tom. I think he mighta been plannin' to go with her, too. I can't imagine she wouldn't tell him, and he wouldn't have let her go all alone, bless his heart.

"That night was ordinary, to begin with. None of us knew Tom was in there with Mamma. It makes me squirm a little to think of it if I'm honest, but I've gotten over it. The first sign of trouble was when Daddy came home. I was in the girls' bedroom, puttin' Idgie, Dolly, and Diamond to bed. We heard Daddy come in, stumble up the stairs, and go down the hall to their room. He was earlier comin' home than he usually was. Next thing he was yellin', but I couldn't pay attention to what he was sayin' because I had to keep the girls from goin' to see what was goin' on. I didn't know myself, but I could guess enough to know it couldn't be good. So I kept them in there, including Diamond. Then Rodney came in with Billy, sayin' he'd seen Daddy pushin' Tom out of their room.

"At that moment when I wasn't lookin', Diamond got the door open as soon as she heard Tom's name. She opened the door just as Daddy was pushin' Tom out and down the stairs. She was ready to go on out after 'em, but Rodney and I held her back. She was screamin' for him, *Good Lord*, she was screamin'. I still hear it in my nightmares sometimes. We managed to get her back, but Rodney must have let her go when I was dealin' with the others. The twins and Billy were all cryin'; they didn't know what was goin' on. And we didn't either. It wasn't until after the first shot a few minutes later that I noticed Diamond managed to sneak away. I was so afraid. I yelled at Rodney for lettin' her go, but it wasn't his fault. I did apologize later on for bein' so mean to him, but I still think he felt guilty. He's travellin' in Europe now, you know, and I'm the only one of us he never sends any postcards too. I don't know where to send a letter to tell him, but I hope he knows I still love him.

"After the first shot, I opened the door and called for her. When I opened it, I saw Mamma knelt on the floor, cryin'. I knelt myself and held her, all the while keepin' an eye on the door, makin' sure the kids stayed in. When I told Mamma I couldn't find Diamond, she came back to herself. She said she was gonna go down and see what was goin' on. She told me to stay and look after the others. So I did as Mamma said, and we all sat on the floor, clingin' to each other. Not long after that, we heard a second shot. I didn't know what to think. I thought Daddy must've killed him.

"I stayed there with them all through the night. We heard the sirens, saw the lights comin' through the window and onto the ceilin'. We were all cryin', and I didn't know what to tell them to make it better. We were all there until the youngins cried themselves to sleep, and me and Rodney lifted 'em up and put them to bed. Diamond was still gone, and I was pretty sure somethin' had happened to her, though I was afraid to think what, so we put Billy in her bed.

"The two of us left the room then, and neither of us was sure if we should go downstairs or not. The police were mostly gone by then; just a couple left that we could see over the railing. Mamma was there talkin' to 'em. She'd stopped cryin' by then, but I'd never seen her look so upset. She noticed us lookin' down, and so did the police officers, and they left. We waited for her to say something, and she gestured for us to come down. When we got down there, she walked us over to the dining table and sat us down.

"That's when she told us that Daddy was dead; that Tom had killed him, and Tuck, too. Then she told us that Diamond had run away, and police were out lookin' for her. I couldn't even be shocked by then; I was so exhausted. It was damn near one in the mornin'. Then Mamma said that the next few weeks weren't gonna be easy, maybe longer than that. She asked us to be brave and said that no matter what happened or what we heard people say, that she loved us so much and hoped that we could forgive her, though she never really said what for.

"That was the night. The rest was a blur, and the only thing I kept feelin' was incomplete. There was no resolution, no nothing. They told us we were gonna get through it, but we were never told much about what happened that night. And they didn't spend a long time lookin' for poor Diamond before they gave up, bunch of dips. And Mamma figured if the child had been so unhappy here even with Tom, she would be miserable without him. She said we had to let her go if we were ever gonna move on."

Banks paused a beat, then asked gently, "But you haven't, have you?"

Eliza paused, taking a breath and allowing another silent tear to fall. She did not appear to be on the verge of any kind of breakdown, but she sat there, thoughtful and mildly vacant, taking in the sad reality that was her September twenty-first, 1955. After just a moment, Eliza reached over to the end table in the corner between the couch and the chair. She opened the drawer, which Banks could see held numerous framed photographs. She took the top one out of the drawer and held it out to Banks.

Banks took it and saw that the black-and-white picture was of a young girl. Banks felt a pull at her heart as she realized the girl was Diamond McMullen, immediately understanding how a person could want to protect her at all costs. The photograph had been taken from the waist up, and the subject was looking at something or someone out of shot. She wore a sweet, white-collared dress that Banks was sure was blue, even though the photograph was color-less. The girl's long, empty left sleeve hung half in shot, half out, but Banks could see through the somewhat sheer material of it that there was nothing there. Diamond's curly and chaotic dark hair and matching dark brows were a stark contrast to her adopted siblings' reddish-blonde tones. The only thing Diamond seemed to share with them was her light eyes. With the big doe eyes and her petite features otherwise, she looked like a baby doll, and, even without a smile on her face, she encompassed childish innocence. Banks knew the child would have been thirteen years old in this photograph, but had she not known, she would have put money on nine or ten years instead.

Who would abandon this poor child? She thought.

There was a twinge of anger in her now, primarily toward Diamond's biological father. Banks was reminded of one of the first cases she had worked, under Wild's supervision, as she stared at the photograph. It had been a missing person case, and the person in question was a young boy named Justin Ford, age eight. Banks remembered the insurmountable pain that she had seen in the parents' eyes as they gave her a description of the boy and any possible place he would have been before he disappeared. They had plastered the whole city of Montgomery in "Have you seen this child?" posters, and Banks had worked day and night to find him as his mother and father prayed for their child to be brought back to them.

Thankfully, though it does not always work out that way, Banks and Wild found the child wandering around the other side of the city. They discovered that someone had kidnapped him and planned to ransom him back to his parents, both from wealthy families. Eventually, the kidnappers had decided there were too many people looking for the boy and that he wasn't worth prison, so they just dropped him off somewhere. Luckily, some weeks later, the boy recognized one of his captors on a day out with his family, and Banks and Wild had ensured that they ended up in prison anyway, where they belonged. When the two detectives had brought the child home to his parents, the looks on their faces shattered Banks' entire being, and it was the one and only time anyone had ever seen a tear fall from Jerry Wild's eye.

Thinking of the love of those parents still made Banks tear up, and now, looking at the photograph of another missing child, Banks felt a wave of determined and robust anger for the man who abandoned the child. Not only him, but anyone who would hurt this child, and whoever the sons of bitches were that gave up looking for her. If she knew that their lack of diligence had had anything to do with Diamond McMullen's disability, Banks would have already been over at the police station in Dothan, demanding to know who was working there in 1955.

Eliza broke the silence as Banks stared at the photograph, trying to keep her emotions to herself.

"Ain't she the most precious thing you ever saw?" She asked in her soft voice, and Banks jumped as she came down from the cloud she had been in. She looked up for a moment to see Eliza smiling with pride, though tears still filled her eyes. Banks removed her anger and frustration as she remembered where she was.

"She is," Banks said, smiling as she looked back down and tried to blink her own tears away. "I'm sure wherever she is, she has grown into a beautiful woman now."

Eliza nodded, also staring at the photo in Banks' hands. Banks looked back up and handed the picture back. Eliza looked at it herself for a moment longer, then put it back in the drawer, shutting it again.

"If I can ask," Banks said, sniffing back emotion, "Why do you keep those pictures in there?"

Eliza sighed. "So they don't stare at me. All those pictures are old, from another life. I know it's silly, but my siblings are all so different now than they were, and even though I can barely face them now, it just puts a hurtin' on my soul to look at them as they were then, before that mess happened.

"It hurts the most to see her." Eliza stared at the closed drawer as she spoke. "I failed her. We all did. The little ones were cruel to her, and I should have taken better care to be sure she had what she wanted. She could have been happy with us, you know. But I let my own childish problems distract me from what she needed. And now she's gone. I didn't know her enough even to know what she would have wanted us to do when she left. When she hadn't come back for a year, and we figured she wasn't goin' to, I plucked one of the roses from the garden and sent it floatin' down the crick a few minutes away. Just as a send-off. No, I can't look at her for too long. She might be out there still, sure. But that little girl could have died out there alone, and it's my fault."

"It's not, Eliza," Banks said. "It's no one's fault Diamond chose to run."

Eliza did not seem to hear Banks' attempt at reassurance. She just sniffed and took a deep breath, closing her eyes. Banks pressed on for the sake of time, but did so delicately, moving on to a different, though similarly bitter subject.

"Were you sad about what happened to your father?" She asked.

Eliza blinked, wiped a couple of tears away, and sighed. "Sure I was. He wasn't the most feeling person you ever met, but he was still my daddy. The funeral was tough for sure, but mostly because of the cause of death and the stuff surrounding it. Daddy's family wouldn't talk to Mamma at all, and we don't talk to them much anymore, either.

"The thing is, us kids got together for Christmas a few years ago, and that's the only time I usually see them besides the Fourth of

July, and we were all sittin' around talkin' about Daddy, and we all kinda came to the same realization. That even though we were sad, Daddy never gave any of us much of his time, so it didn't hurt as much as it probably should have when he was killed."

"Going along with that," Banks said, continuing the interrogation. "What about now? Do you feel differently about the event or any of the other circumstances after you've had time to think about it?"

"Well, I have a bad habit of blamin' myself," Eliza said. "I wondered whether if I hadn't hurt Tom so bad, he would have been on that path in the first place. Or maybe I should have shot him down earlier instead of entertainin' the idea of love, then neither one of us might've been hurtin' so bad. And I always think about how stupid it was to go kissin' Tuck in the barn. Wasn't any good reason for it; I was just actin' out. But I can't help thinkin' I led him to his fate."

"Eliza," Banks consoled sternly, "Tom didn't kill Tuck because of what you did. The attorney thought he shot him because he was a witness, but I'm starting to think he was comin' after Tom, too, and Tom defended himself. Do you think he would kill someone over something like that? And also, that whole thing between you and Tom was not all your fault. You were both so young; neither of you knew how to handle your emotions."

Eliza looked at her with some gratitude this time. "Thank you, Detective," she said. "What was your first name, again?"

"Isla," Banks told her. "Isla Banks."

"Isla," Eliza repeated. "Thank you, Isla."

Banks smiled at her, and Eliza returned it in kind. Eliza was a sweet person, despite being a little misguided and severely traumatized. She was certainly very open to the conversation once it got going, and was generous to give Banks her time, just like Idgie had been. Regardless of what ended up happening, Violet McMullen had, at the very least, raised her children to be compassionate and polite. Even with the weight of the past dragging them down and always trying to hold them back.

As Banks was thinking about this, something else occurred to her, and she immediately sought counsel on it.

"Eliza, your mamma," she said. "You said she went downstairs, there was some time, and then you heard the second shot. I'm almost wondering—"

"—If Mamma shot one of 'em," Eliza finished for her, not the least surprised. "Yeah, I've wondered that, myself. I don't wanna believe it, but then again, I never wanted to believe Tom could do it, either. Sometimes even the people you know the most are a mystery to you."

"And have you decided how probable it is that she would have?" Banks asked.

Eliza took a second to think before she answered. "It could be. I think there's a decent possibility, and I don't think I'd be all that surprised. Not a whole lot surprises me anymore. I will say that I don't think she'd do it for no reason. There'd need to be something happening for her to step in."

Interesting, Banks thought.

"Eliza," Banks inquired, "I've been wondering where the gun came into the picture. Do you have any idea of its journey that night? Could Tom have had it when they went downstairs?"

Eliza took another moment, attempting to recall. "I don't think so," she said. "I didn't look at Daddy, though. Maybe he took it from Tom, with the plan of killin' him for what he'd done." As hot as it was outside, Eliza appeared to have a slight chill after that sentence. "I don't know where else it could have come from unless Tuck had it."

"Hmm," Banks pondered. "Yes, Tuck may have stolen the gun from Tom's house, and he would have had the motive to kill Tom, in his own twisted reasoning. It is possible."

"Maybe Tom wrestled it away from him?" Eliza asked, on the edge of her seat.

"That wouldn't work with the placing," Banks decided. "Tom and Tuck had to be on opposite sides for him to have shot them.

Unless..." Banks' brain was on fire. Her head felt so full it might explode. "What if Tuck *missed*? What if he was aiming for Tom but killed your dad instead?"

"Oh!" Eliza exclaimed, looking more invested than she had the entire time they had spoken. "And maybe Mamma went down there, and got him to drop the gun, because he was caught, and then Tom picked it up and shot him! Or maybe Mamma got him to give it to her, and then *she* shot Tuck because he killed Daddy, or because he was trying to kill Tom!"

Banks smiled wide at Eliza, who smiled back at her. Banks thought the two of them must have looked looney, sitting there in that plain house, almost shouting about murder.

"That could be," Banks said. "It checks out, for sure. I mean, I'd need more concrete evidence, but that's the closest I've gotten to a full picture. The only thing missing is Diamond."

"Yeah," Eliza said, settling back down to think, though still radiating youthful energy that she had had no trace of just a minute earlier. "I don't think she left without checking it out first. And if she was there, Mamma could have been holdin' her back, to keep her out of the crossfire. Mamma's a fierce woman about protecting her children. That's how we were in the dark about the details for so long."

It made sense. It all made sense. Banks made a silent reminder to thank Wild when she saw him for the idea to talk to Eliza Miller in the first place. Banks said farewell to Eliza, making sure to tell her what she had told Idgie, in case they spoke, and left that plain house, finally feeling like she had something to work with.

~ 14 ~

HOW THE TABLES HAVE TURNED

SATURDAY, AUGUST 21, 1965. 08:07 AM.

"You're in good spirits today, Detective."

Banks looked across the interrogation table at Tom, who looked at her with an amused expression on his face. She was, indeed, in excellent spirits today because she finally felt like their conversation would not be a mystery anymore. She had thought a million times over about the theory she and Eliza had come up with, and she was more and more convinced that it was true. Now she needed matching testimony and likely some tangible evidence to change the game.

"I am, Tom," she said. "It's always the highlight of my week to see you."

Tom's smile expanded even more, and he rolled his eyes like a schoolgirl. "Detective, you're gonna make me blush. Speakin' of blushin', should I tell you more about what happened after me and Mrs. got together?"

"You absolutely should," Banks said, smiling freely in anticipation.

* * *

So you were right, we got together again. We got together a lot. Every time we did it, Mrs. McMullen would say we shouldn't, I would agree, and then we would do it anyway. Just imagine if Betty and I had continued even after sayin' we shouldn't. Her daddy probably woulda killed me on the spot, no questions asked. Guess I wouldn't be here, though.

The worst part of the whole thing was that we would do what we were doin', but then Mrs. McMullen would always go on about the problems in her life and her marriage, and I certainly learned a lot. I already told ya he went out all the time, but that wasn't the worst part. Mrs. told me that her husband didn't always come back 'til mornin', but if he did, he'd be all drunk and strange-actin', and he'd be wantin' her bad. And even if she was sleepin', he'd wake her up wantin' some fun. She said she usually didn't want to, but she did it anyway. Now, I knew that was wrong, so I asked her one night if I should stay until he got there and fight him off her if he tried anythin'. She just smiled and said it wouldn't do no good. Even if it worked once, he'd just try again next time. To him, it was his right.

Now, knowin' this, every time I saw the man for those couple weeks, I'd be feelin' so angry. And even though he never spoke to me, I wouldn't nod to him when passin' by as I'd done before, I barely looked at him. It was my way of rebellin' just a little, even though he probably didn't notice it.

Betty noticed somethin' was up with me, too. I was real different there for a while, not speakin' to anybody but the boys I did work with. One day, she found me when I was takin' a break from workin' to sit in the shade of the barn. She asked me if I'd been feelin' alright.

"Best I ever felt, Miss Betty," I said, "Ain't nothin' the matter, don't worry."

She just looked at me with them wide eyes and said, "You're lyin', Tom Higgins. There is somethin' the matter, I know it. You've been so quiet."

She was right, of course. I said, "Well, maybe I'm just tired, you know. Lots of work to do around this time."

Miss Betty still knew somethin' was up, and she just didn't wanna rest until I fessed up. "Tom, if this is about what happened," she said, "I'm really sorry. I acted like a fool. Please forgive me; I won't be able to live with myself if you don't."

I said, "Miss Betty, ain't nothin' to forgive. I've moved on from it, so don't you go thinkin' too much about it, now. We's square."

You know, for a minute there, I *really* thought I wasn't feelin' for her anymore. I had things to keep secret, but it didn't hurt so much to see her anymore. My answer then seemed to satisfy her enough to stop askin' me questions, but I felt terrible lyin' to her, and even more so knowin' what I'd been doin' with her mamma. I didn't know I was also feelin' bad because I was still feelin' for her.

The only thing that gave me peace was knowin' I wouldn't be around much longer to keep causin' them trouble. When I'd come out of Mrs.' room those nights I was with her, careful not to let anyone know I was there, Miss Diamond would sneak out and meet me out back on the porch, and we'd talk a little. We was still plannin' on runnin' away. We didn't tell nobody about it and wasn't plannin' to. We was also tryin' to figure out how to go without it seemin' like I was kidnappin' here or somethin'. Obviously, you know we didn't end up needin' that plan. Little did we know...

I had thought for a while of makin' it look like I got sick and died like poor Ricky, but I figured I'd have to get someone to tell the McMullens because I wouldn't be able to tell them myself. And if I said I was sick, the boys would come out lookin' for me, and they'd know I wasn't. Just sayin' I was leavin' wouldn't work, neither. It was too close to the truth.

What we thought would be the best idea was pretendin' an accident, like fallin' off somethin'. It'd have to be somewhere there wouldn't be a body, though, like a crick or somethin'. There's one of them about ten minutes away from the orchard. It's down the road and through them woods across from where my house is. Miss Diamond said she'd do it, but we didn't know how we was gonna justify her bein' that far away. Plus, if she was alone, she'd have to make her way back alone, and she didn't know those parts like I do, and I was afraid she'd get lost.

We decided we needed someone else to be witness to it, or maybe two. The two boys I trusted the most there was Johnnie and Jimmy, so I asked them to do it. You know, it's real nice that Johnnie never told anyone about this, 'specially since he's in with the family now. Guess I ain't surprised, though. When y'ain't got money or nothin' of value to make deals with, all you got's your word. He told me he wouldn't tell; they both did. They kept their word. Whenever I get out of here, I owe them a whole lot. Wonder where Jimmy is...

They didn't want to at first, though. When I asked 'em, Jimmy nearly had a heart attack, poor fella.

He said, "You're leavin? What are we gonna do without you around?"

I said, "Aw, man, you'll be alright. We all gotta move on from this place sooner or later."

Then Johnnie said, "Where do you think y'all are goin'?"

I didn't have an answer to give him, so I just told him, "Some-where where it ain't s'damn hot."

They both laughed at that. Jimmy and Johnnie was good ol' boys, I tell ya.

So here was the plan: Me and the boys would go out to the crick out there around the middle of the day when we usually took a break. They would say we were goin' out there to cool off from the hot day. The real reason we went out there was so the time would be right, just in case someone had their eye on a watch when we did it. They also went out there with me so we could say our goodbyes. They were the closest thing to friends I had, along with Miss Diamond. I sure miss 'em.

Anyway, so when we got out there, I'd have a little head start, I'd go by my house one last time, and get just a couple things: some clothes, a couple of pictures, a pistol, and I put 'em all in the only bag I had. Meanwhile, the boys would go back yellin' and screamin' that I'd drowned. That crick out there's real deep, and when the police would go out to look for me, they'd give up after a little. It's not like they'd've had any of my family to answer to. The funny thing was: when they went and told the McMullens, no cops ever got sent out. I imagine Mr. McMullen didn't think it was worth it, or maybe he'd noticed how I was behavin' different and thought I was disrespectful. I don't know.

So they did the plan exactly like we'd said, and I found a spot in the woods to hide until the sun was settin'. I walked through the woods and the farm fields to get back to the orchard so that I wouldn't run into the boys on the road. The plan was that I'd be out there waitin' for Miss Diamond to sneak out after everyone else was sleepin'. So I went into the rows, careful to be quiet, and hid out of sight.

I know what you're thinkin', now. What could have gone wrong here? The plan was set. All I had to do was wait. And I did, for a bit. But then I started to feel guilty about Mrs. McMullen, and how upset she'd probably be about me, then how upset she'd be when Miss Diamond went missin'. I figured if she knew we were both safe, at least she wouldn't be hurtin' so bad. I was worried she wouldn't let us go, but I thought it was the right thing to do to tell her.

So that's what I did. I figured I had time until Miss Diamond thought it was safe to sneak away, and I'd been watchin' the house for a bit, and no one was stirrin'. Mr. McMullen's car hadn't been in the drive, and I was pretty well acquainted with his night habits by now, so I snuck in the house, quiet as a mouse. I crept up the stairs and went down to Mrs. McMullen's room. I knocked real quiet, hopin' she'd hear. Luckily, or maybe not so luckily, she did.

She opened the door and looked like she was seein' a ghost since she probably thought she was. I put a hand on her mouth so she didn't scream and waited for her to cool down a bit so I could let her go. She brought me in the room, and we were whisperin' to each other. The room looked so different in the lamplight. I'd only really been in there when it was dark.

So I told her everything. I told her how we had faked my death and all and that me and Miss Diamond was plannin' on runnin' away. She said she hadn't even told the children about my 'accident' yet, since they'd been at school when it happened, and she went on about how happy she was that I was alive. Mrs. was a little upset by the whole thing, of course. And when I say a little, I mean she was bawlin' her eyes out—poor thing. I had to keep tellin' her to hush, so no one would hear and come in to check on her. Eventually, she calmed down, and she told me I had her blessing to take Miss Diamond, even though she'd miss us both terribly.

That's when everything went wrong.

I tried to leave, Detective, believe me. I didn't wanna leave her so upset, but I knew I needed to get outta there. She jumped on me, I promise. I'm not makin' excuses, either. I've already told you I'm as guilty with that situation as she was, and obviously, I'm not tryna convince anyone of my virtuosity, but this time she just would not let me go, and I couldn't bring myself to force her away from me. She was all up on me, kissin' me and all, and goin' for more. It was durin' all that I noticed an empty bottle of wine on her nightstand. She took my shirt off me and was goin' for my pants. I was wonderin' if we still had time...

And then I heard footsteps comin' up the hall.

I tried to get her off me, but there was no time. So I turned us so I was on top of her, makin' me look like the problem to save her dignity. I figured if it looked like I was in control, she wouldn't get in any trouble (Although, by the way, they never wanted to talk to her about anything that happened because they thought she was some kinda hussy. Ain't nothin' but bullshit, Detective, but I'm sure you know that). That's when Mr. McMullen busted in the door. He started yellin' and all. Sayin' how he was gonna kill me. I jumped off Mrs. McMullen and stood to face him.

And the rest is stuff you've heard before. We went out into the hall, and he was pushin' me along. The kids had all heard the commotion, and one of the bedroom doors opened. Miss Diamond was trying to get out of the grip of Miss Betty and Rodney. She was screamin'. I ain't never heard her scream before, not for anything. She was callin' for me, and I looked up at Miss Betty. I'll never forget the horror in her eyes. That moment we'd been fearin' had come, and we'd never even had a chance to love each other.

I didn't have any time to say anything because I had to focus on not fallin' down the stairs, the way he was pushin' me. He sure was strong when he was drunk, ol' McMullen. But I figured I could take him since I was sober and would be able to move a little quicker.

We got out there to the barn, and I was tryin' to get my bearings, but he didn't give me a second before he started wailin' on me. He sure got me good, too. You gotta remember, too, I still didn't have a shirt on, so he hit me right on my skin, and rings he was wearin' cut me all up. I was fightin' back, but he had such a fury, and I just remember he smelled real strong of smoke and whiskey.

I'd almost started slippin' away when I finally managed to get away from him enough to... well, you know. I shot twice, but he was already half fallen after the first one—second one-hit Tuck, who was standin' by the entrance of the barn. I'd heard his footsteps, and when I saw it was him, I knew he'd get me once I did what I had to. If the second bullet hadn't hit him, I woulda shot again. I knew I couldn't let him go after seein' what I did, as awful as that makes me.

~ 15 ~

SHOOTING HERSELF IN THE FOOT

08:31 AM.

"And that's pretty much the story, Detective," Tom said, taking a deep breath and looking down at the table in front of him. "I tried to run, threw the gun away, and got about half a mile down the road before collapsin'. Ol' Mr. McMullen did me up real bad, and even if I kept moving, I was droppin' blood enough for them to follow. You know the rest."

Banks let out a breath that she hadn't known she had been holding. When Tom stopped speaking, he looked up at her, waiting for her to say something. She furrowed her brows, as the only thing she could feel at the conclusion she had been waiting for was confusion.

"That... that was what happened?" She asked.

"Yeah, that pretty much sums it up," Tom answered, although Banks noticed that he was not smiling anymore.

"Okay," Banks said, thrown off her rhythm, "so where was the gun?"

Tom sighed, seeming like he was trying not to be upset about something. "I told you, I got it from my house before," he said, "I had it with me."

Banks was put off by his change in attitude, but she continued, growing somewhat irritated all the while. "I thought it was in your bag. That's what you said. Did you really have time to grab it before going down to the barn?"

Tom faltered, and for a moment, there was something different beneath the surface, but he squashed it back down and held himself up. Banks tried not to look annoyed.

It can't be, she kept thinking. *It just can't be.*

"Are you lying, Tom?" She asked quietly. "Please say you're lying."

Tom held back his feelings, but not without visible effort. Banks had never seen him so upset, even when he spoke about Betty, or Diamond's past, which were the only other times he seemed at all bothered. Now, he was a different person. Tortured and alone, but also... could it be? Afraid?

Regardless of the feelings fighting him, he spoke clearly, in just as quiet a voice as Banks had used.

"Detective," he almost whispered. "The only one lyin' here is you. I overheard one of the guards say the cops reopened my case. Then I heard them say it was closed again. That was the week you took so long to come back, and I figured that was it." He took another deep breath and looked into Banks' eyes, flashing her back to her dreams. "Yet here you are. I figured you seemed interested in the story, so I told it. I knew we'd get here, and I think you knew that, too. Never understood what made you so interested in it. So what are you doin' here, *Detective?*"

Tom had put a particular stinging emphasis on the word, 'Detective,' swiftly removing any friendliness that had existed between them with no more than a word. Now it was Banks who thought she might cry. She wasn't sure what to say, so she told the truth.

"You're right, Tom," she said, desperately attempting to keep an even tone. "They reopened your case. The victory model was found in a bayou in Louisiana almost three months ago. I convinced them there might be something under the surface, so I asked them to re-

open it on the grounds that the new evidence might bring something to light."

Tom took in a sharp breath but did not speak. Banks continued.

"After just a little while, they decided it wasn't worth it to continue investigating. I begged them to give me a chance, but they
refused. I told them there was more to this story; I was sure of it.
This was the one chance I had to show them that my judgment
is worth trusting. I threw myself into this case, hoping something
would come to fruition and make my efforts worth it.

"Over these weeks, Tom, my interest in your story has only
grown. I have listened to you speak about how much you care about
the people around you, about Betty, about Diamond. And not just
you. I talked to Idgie and Betty, too. They care about you too, Tom.
They can't believe you would shoot someone, no matter how in
danger you were. I even visited your house. Whether either of us
likes it or not, I'm invested in your story, and not only that. I've become invested in you, Tom. And I have decided that I can't believe
you would do it, either."

Banks' train of thought was going without her. Her heart gave
her mind no time to defend. This was precisely what she tried to
avoid when she noticed a personal connection forming. The front
was compromised, and Banks did not even try to strategize before
waving a white flag in the air.

"So if you're going to sit here and tell me that everyone is wrong,
that I'm wrong, and you are the monster that the attorney made you
out to be, then I don't know what I can say. I thought you were a
good man, Tom. I was willing to bet on it. But if you're telling me
that there is no more to it, then you're the worst there is. You trick
people into loving you, and you ruin everything for them. If that's
who Tom Higgins is, you deserve to be here, even if you didn't shoot
anyone.

"Please," Banks gave herself away with the tear that was cur-
rently falling down the side of her face. "Please, Tom. Tell me you're
lying so I can work to get you out of here. Tell me there's more."

Tom kept a straight face as he stared at her. When she'd said her piece, he said, "I'm sorry to disappoint you, Detective. I guess I am what they say I am, after all. If you had been payin' attention from the beginnin' like you thought you was, you would know exactly the kind of man I am."

9:03 AM.

Banks was trying to keep herself together, now sat in her Bel-Air, driving back home.

Ripley had noticed something was wrong when Banks was the one who tapped the glass, and even more so if he had seen the tears that Banks was fervently trying to keep from view. She was sure he would be gossiping with his office lady friend about it, but Banks didn't care. She wouldn't be going back there, anyway.

She couldn't help but feel foolish. After everything she had seen and heard, this outcome was what Banks feared the most. She put everything on the line: her career, her professionalism, and most unadvisedly, her heart. And while she still had her job, *for now*, everything else was compromised. It felt like her chest was on fire, burning until it consumed her.

It should not have been hurting this bad. Banks was a professional detective. She had seen cases of this nature and closed them with no conflicting feelings. Usually, if a theory or lead fell through, it was irritating, sure, but never personal. An anomaly was occurring, and Banks cursed the name of Tom Higgins for whatever he had done to her, hoping and praying that this would not affect the procedure for cases in the future.

As she was midthought, Banks suddenly snapped to attention, realizing that she was driving in the wrong direction. This realization thrust upon her after passing the picture-perfect Hale and Pritchett Orchard.

Banks rolled her eyes. *Fantastic,* she thought.

Not in any hurry to return home, especially since she no longer had any specific purpose she wanted to indulge when she got there, Banks continued driving toward Tom's house. She was not planning to go there, but rather, she had a different place that she wanted to see if this was indeed the last time she would need to be in this area of Dothan.

Banks had a feeling that she was losing her mind. For one, nobody hikes in the woods wearing oxfords or slacks. But with defeat having put its anchor down in her chest, she figured the image of her current activity hardly mattered.

She had pulled over across from Tom's house and began walking into the woods on the other side. There was no path in these woods, so it was a rough beginning. After an early struggle wrestling with loose twigs and roots, Banks maneuvered herself further, careful with every step. Thankfully the creek was not too far from the road, because Banks had not considered the time and distance of the little details she had to go off of. After just a few minutes of walking, she came to a ledge, and the steep slope down led to water.

It was almost peaceful enough there to forget about the August humidity. Birds were singing in the trees above, and the creek below flowed along and gave off its own serene melody. Banks thought about how nice it would be to come here with Tom...

Stop it, she thought.

Forcing herself to return to her senses, she examined the water below, trying not to get too close to the ledge for fear she may slip. It was at least fifteen feet down, and the water *did* seem deep for a creek. The water itself was murky, hiding its contents from the light of day. Not only that, but as she looked side to side, she saw that the creek extended beyond her view, twisting around in a cavernous path indented in the earth.

As she looked down, the sun emerged from behind a small cloud, and the light moved across the woods gradually. Banks watched as the light glittered across the surface of the water below. Just then, there was another glimmer of light reflected outside of the water, and it drew banks' attention to the narrow shore, where the creek was lapping water to the side. Banks pushed her glasses up and knelt down, trying to get a better look. It was a tiny speck and appeared to be metal, but that was all she could discern.

I could survive that fall, right?

After an admittedly short time considering, Banks searched the area for an easy way down. She found a spot that seemed the safest available, though it still wasn't ideal as, say, a staircase. Banks turned away and, putting her hands down for anchored support, lowered her leg to a rooted branch some feet down, as though going down a ladder.

Ledge by precarious ledge, Banks slowly lowered herself down into the miniature ravine. By the time Banks' oxfords made contact with the damp dirt at the bottom, her heart was beating fast due to many near slips. She let her other foot come down and stepped to a large rock on the edge of the water for more secure ground. Standing at the edge, she could extend her arm out and touch the sloping wall. She rested her heart for a moment and looked to the ground for the metal piece.

She locked eyes on it, just a few feet in front of her. She stepped from rock to rock until she was able to bend down and reach it. When she brushed the damp sand from it and examined it in her hand, she realized that it was a slender bullet, and it was rusty, but it maintained a surprising amount of shine, given the long time it seemed to have been there.

Instantly, Banks wondered if it connected to Tom's case, but as defeated as she was feeling and as much motivation as she was lacking, she decided to pocket it and consider it later. A moment passed as she thought of her situation, and it was then that she looked up and realized how deep in she was.

I should have thought about that before I came down here, she thought.

WEDNESDAY, AUGUST 25, 1965. 07:42 PM.

The next few days flew by, and Banks hardly noticed. She tried desperately to put herself in her work, working with Wild to solve the robbery case, solving it, making arrests, getting confessions, filling out paperwork. It could have been a satisfying victory once the case was closed and trial impending, and it should have been. Banks tried hard to be happy, but Wild, *ever* the expert on *feelings* of *any* kind, noticed the change in his partner's behavior.

The two of them were sitting at Easy's Bar the Wednesday after Banks' last visit to Tom, having a small celebratory drink upon completing their latest case. At that moment, Banks was staring into her cosmopolitan, thinking about how guilty she was that she had barely been in on the solving of this case because she had been busy, pointlessly gallivanting around Dothan. Wild looked over to her, sipped on his old fashioned, and brought her out of her trance.

"Are you doin' alright, Banks?" He asked her.

She jumped a little, having been deep in thought. She looked over to see Wild's eyebrows raised, waiting for her to respond. She sighed.

"I guess," she said. "It's so stupid, Wild. I'm still caught up on this Higgins thing."

She looked back down into her drink, and Wild thought for a moment before offering anything else. After a few more thoughtful sips, he spoke again.

"You know," he said, "this isn't the only case you'll have that's like this."

Banks rolled her eyes at her drink. "Very reassuring, Wild. Thank you."

"No, it's not like that," he said. "I just mean that you shouldn't feel bad for getting hung up on a case. It don't make you any worse of a detective for feeling defeated when something doesn't work out. It's not always easy-going, movin' on."

Banks sat up in her seat, taking a sip of her own drink, instead of just staring at it. She looked over to Wild, who was patiently waiting for her to say something.

"I know," she said. "I'm just worried that it ain't the *case* itself that's weighing on my mind. I made it personal, Wild. And now I'm ruined for it."

"Well," Wild said, "that happens, too. You know, some of my first cases broke me. I've seen a killer walk free and an innocent man put to death. I've seen God's children tortured and killed, and the perpetrator never found. I've sat in that station all night, prayin' for a miracle, wonderin' why I was in this job if I wasn't good enough to finish what I started.

"This job ain't never just about the office work, it ain't about the hours, it ain't about the paycheck. You do the best you can do, and sometimes it don't work out the way you want it. Sometimes the families of innocent victims haunt you in your dreams, and all you can do is try to remind yourself that you did all you could do. You can be as professional as you can muster, but any human would feel for people whose life hasn't served them well. But it ain't your fault. You can only do so much."

Banks sat in awe as Wild spoke to her soul. It was easy for her, most of the time, to shut out encouragement or consolation if she didn't think she deserved it, but she never expected something like that from Jerry Wild, of all people.

"Geez, Wild," she said. "I didn't know you cared so much about this stuff."

He shrugged. "I try not to, anymore," he said. "It's easier to go to sleep at night if you don't. But the world always needs people who do care. And you care a hell of a lot about justice, Banks. That's why this is so tough for you."

Banks took another sip. "I just wish there had been some closure. It still feels like there's *more*, but I'll never get to the end of it."

Wild took another sip, too. "Maybe there *is* more."

"But it doesn't matter. Tom won't say anymore, and the case is kaput anyway. There's no more to be had."

"You said he was upset, though, didn't you? You thought he was hiding something. If you dig, you could find it."

"Wild," Banks looked over to him, and she found herself smiling again, "are you suggesting I continue this case, against direct orders, with no leads to speak of?"

"I'm not suggesting," he said, offering a small smile in return. "I'm beggin' you."

Banks' smile was short-lived because just then, she remembered a crucial detail. "Well, I can't dig too far. Sarge locked up the case files and the notes I had in there from earlier on. I've been runnin' on testimony and my personal notes, but to get somewhere with this, I'm gonna need to go through those files again."

Banks was expecting Wild to give up on the issue, but she noticed that his smile had not budged when she finished speaking.

"Well, then," he said, "then it's a damn good thing I locked them up in my desk instead of in the archived files."

Banks furrowed her brows and stared at him. "You did *what?*"

He looked as amused as his face would allow him. "The Sarge gave me a bunch of files to lock in the archive, and I noticed the name, 'Higgins,' on one of them. I knew you were doing the case without permission by then, so I figured you might need them at some point. See? That's what happens when you're patient and quiet. No one sees you as a threat."

"Jerry Wild," Banks said, smiling and lifting her glass. "It's always a pleasure working with you."

"And you, Isla Banks," Wild raised his glass, and they toasted to working under the radar.

SATURDAY, AUGUST 28, 1965. 10:15 PM.

Even with Wild's support, Banks could not help but feel overwhelmed by everything. She was not sure how she wanted to proceed to investigate beyond just going through court records, evidence, and her notes again and again until something connected. It was a desperate method, but at least there was no time to contend with.

The one thing that lived in Banks' mind at all times was Tom's last remark he made to her.

If you had been payin' attention from the beginnin' like you thought you was, he had said, *you would know exactly the kind of man I am.*

Well, Banks *had* been paying attention; there was no question in her mind. She had relived and stressed over every detail she had access to, and never, not once could she remember earnestly believing that the outcome to his testimony was the whole truth. She could admit to herself that she was caught in her feelings which, she could no longer deny, had been growing every time she had visited Tom Higgins. However, even after considering this and running through her timeline again, things still did not add up.

Banks sat on the floor of her apartment on Saturday night, when she would have been reviewing new notes from a conversation with Tom if their relationship had not gone sour. There was the sound of papers being frantically shuffled around, as well as the radio playing. They were playing the Rolling Stones', "(I Can't Get No) Satisfaction," and Banks chuckled a little when it came on because it was as though Mick Jagger himself could see how she was feeling about all of the case details scattered around her brain, as well as her floor.

There were a few things that she noticed about the court report. None of which were anything concrete, but they were reasons to keep fighting.

"So I did as he told me, and he took me out to the barn."
"The barn you shot him in?"
"The only barn on the premises, yes, sir."

Every time the attorney or anyone else asked him to confess, Tom danced around saying either yes or no when it concerned the act itself. He always used a roundabout answer instead of a clear one.

I never planned a murder.

Fine. But you did commit one, didn't you? Planned or not, you committed murder that night.

With all due respect, he was beating me, sir.

There it was again. The attorney had tried a couple of times to get a clean confession out of him, but Tom did not oblige. He must have known that his word was only worth so much, so what was the motivation to avoid confessing to the crime?

So why did you have the gun on you in the first place, Mr. Higgins? You had gone to the house that night to be with Mrs. McMullen. You didn't, perhaps, plan on shooting her, too?

No, sir, I would never. She never did anything wrong to anyone.

Well, that was one thing, at least. If Tom had been telling the truth about the runaway plan, then at least Banks now knew why he had the gun with him. She still was not sure Tom would have had time, or a moment Mr. McMullen was not looking to grab the gun from his bag, but then why was answered, at least. Then again, why did Tom keep the plan to run away secret from everyone else but had chosen to divulge it to Banks?

You're a murderer, aren't you, son?

It would seem so, sir.

Now, there was a clear enough answer to satisfy the attorney, but it was still not a yes. Banks wished, once again, that she could have seen that exchange between the attorney and Tom. She wished she could have seen him answer, or at least hear his tone, for maybe there was something more apparent there.

It was now that Banks began to look into her notes again, searching for a sign. She then remembered that she had failed to take any notes during her conversation with Eliza Miller, so she tried hard to think of significant points there. The alternative conclusion the two of them had come up with was reasonable and could still be true, but Banks unsure how to prove it.

"I was so afraid. I opened the door and called for her. When I opened it, I saw Mamma knelt on the floor, cryin'. I knelt myself and held her, all the while keepin' an eye on the door, makin' sure the kids stayed in. When I told Mamma I couldn't find Diamond, she came back to herself. She said she was gonna go down and see what was goin' on. She told me to look after the others. So I did as Mamma said, and we all sat on the floor, clingin' to each other. Not long after that, we heard a second shot. I didn't know what to think. I thought Daddy must've killed him."

Hold on, now. Banks thought. All of that happened after the first shot and before the second. Both the attorney and Tom had said that the two shots had been in immediate procession, one happening right after the other. That couldn't be true because if Eliza remembered correctly, there had been time for her to go out of the room, see her mother, comfort her, and tell her Diamond was missing. Then Violet had time to go downstairs and for young Betty to go back into the room and crouch together with the rest of the children before the second shot sounded. There could only have been one shot before that time; otherwise, they would have heard it.

Why would Tom go along with that story if it couldn't be true?

That was the biggest question of all. Tom was compromising himself on purpose, that much was clear. The real story could not have been any worse than what the attorney had come up with, so it was not for the sake of further incrimination that Tom was lying about the timing and the circumstances. So why?

Banks took in a sharp breath and felt her face become hot. The thought that had sprung into her mind just then filled her with empathetic sorrow.

Does Tom think he deserves to be there? Could he have lied about the committal of second-degree murder to punish himself?

The concept itself was upsetting enough, but then Banks remembered her last parting words to him just the other day in the solitary confinement cell.

"If that's really who you are, then you deserve to be here even if you didn't shoot anyone."

She took her glasses off and dabbed her eyes. Why hadn't she considered that before? Even without the murders, the way he always talked about hurting the people he loved, it was clear he was ashamed of himself. Perhaps he thought this was his penance for forgetting himself. Or even, since the murders happened one way or another, maybe he felt guilty about Diamond going off alone when he promised he'd protect her.

Banks wished she could speak to him. Even if she went to the penitentiary, he could reject her visitation, and she did not want to force him, though she was able.

While she sat in deep concentration, the voice of the radio DJ bled through her consciousness. He announced the next track, and once again, Banks felt like he was reading her mind.

"Good evening all, I hope y'all are doing well this evening. On a night like this, you might be there with your sweetheart, or maybe you are missing someone very special to you. For all you bleeding

*hearts, this one's for you. Here's the Righteous
Brothers with 'Unchained Melody.'"*

Banks sat back against the recliner, listening to the painstak-
ingly familiar and melancholy song, and allowed herself to just
breathe for a moment. She had no choice but to accept that she had
fallen in love with Tom Higgins, though she wasn't sure if it was the
idea of him or the man himself that held her heart captive. It frustrated her to know that she had allowed a personal connection to
affect her work, but she no longer saw a point in hiding it from herself.

As Banks lay in bed that night, the floors of her apartment covered with papers and her typically tidy home in disarray, she felt
how this case was breaking her.

Should I just let it go? She thought. *At this point, it's becoming un-
healthy. I'm far too invested, and it might be clouding my judgment. It isn't
nothing, what I've concluded, but it is enough to be worth doing anything
about it?*

She retreated within herself and fell asleep, thinking of the
storm in Tom Higgins' eyes when she left him in that cell.

~ 16 ~

VIOLETS ARE BLUE

* * *

The Sun is setting on the horizon. The ocean glitters in the afternoon light, peaceful and full of life. There is a boat floating out to sea, and she is in it. She does not row, but the vessel moves on its own, smoothly drifting away from shore. She knows how she got there. She is floating but not lost. She is looking for someone.

As she drifts further and further out, the sunset becomes moonlight, and she can no longer see the shore behind her, though she knows it is there. Something in the water becomes visible, floating at the surface. She wills the boat to approach it. As she comes closer, she can see a person working hard to keep their head above water. This young man has a familiar face.

She comes even closer and attempts, as she has before, to call out to him, but he does not see her. He is looking down at the water just below his chin, panting as he keeps himself from drowning. He looks around frantically for help, but his eyes go past her boat, unable to see her there. She tries to call out again, but to no avail.

She is right next to him now and sees that he is looking down past the water, under it. She leans over the side of her boat to see what he is looking at, but can still see nothing in the dark ocean. She sees how upset he is, and she knows that she desperately wants to help him. He has lost something beneath the water.

She does not think about how deep the ocean is. She does not care. She dives over the side of her boat and into the murky depths. She is not surprised this time to find that she is breathing fine underwater. Swimming ever lower, she searches for what has been lost.

When she is so deep that she can no longer see the moonlight above, there is a soft green glow at the bottom. She knows that this is where the lost item is. Pushing onward, she eventually makes out the shape of a child in the dim glow. Seeing that the child is alone at the bottom of the ocean, she pushes even harder to reach them. The child wears a blue dress, her long, dark hair hangs suspended in the water around her, and her complexion is pale and ghostly. The woman can see the child's face clearly now, and it is a face she has seen before. Her eyes are closed, and her mouth hangs open, unconscious. This young girl has been down here for a long time.

The protagonist knows not to reach for the girl's left arm, so she goes for the right, and the child opens her eyes. Her lifeless pupils stare at the woman, and not a moment later, the child chokes and shakes as she begins to drown. Without hesitation this time, the woman grabs the girl and pushes with her feet on the ocean floor, using all her might as she attempts to save the child from drowning.

As they travel upward, the two great white sharks are swimming in a circle above them. The woman would have been afraid, but she is not going to let this child die. The woman does not look at the sharks as she swims directly through their circle. They do not attack right away, but they follow.

The woman is swimming, too slowly, to the ocean's surface. As they approach, the woman looks down to see the child still alive and fighting, and she thinks she might make it. But just when they are about to break through, and the woman can see the face of the boy, who watches hopefully as they approach him, a powerful force lurches the child from out of the woman's grasp, pulling her back down to the bottom.

The woman stares down as the two sharks pull the girl back down to the bottom. She screams the child's name...

* * *

SUNDAY, AUGUST 29, 1965. 04:11 AM.

Banks awoke once again from a startlingly vivid dream. Tears were falling down her cheeks before she came to, but now she found herself openly sobbing as the sun began to peek through her bedroom window. This was the second time she'd had this dream, which was feeling more and more like a nightmare. This time, the details had been clearer, and it had felt so real that Banks still felt like she was underwater.

In a way, Banks *was* still underwater. She had let herself be enveloped entirely by Tom Higgins' life and in the feelings and events of the Dothan McMullens. She felt a startling empathy flowing through her until it was almost unbearable.

I have to finish this, she thought.

TUESDAY, AUGUST 31, 1965. 09:01 AM.

"Banks, you look awful."

Isla Banks shot to attention, having nearly dozed off, sitting at her work desk. She looked up to see Wild standing over her, with his typical minuscule eyebrow raise, clearly as concerned for her as he could muster. Banks had to take a moment to clock what he had said to her before she could manage an appropriate response.

"Yeah, well, I don't feel so hot, either," she said, looking from Wild down to the papers in front of her, and she could not even remember what she had been doing with them. "I was up half the night. Trying to work all my regular work plus," she looked around to see if any nosy neighbors were listening in, "*the other one* is eating away at me."

Once Wild was satisfied that his partner was not dying at her desk, we went back over to sit at his desk. "I gotta say," he said, "you're always very passionate about things, but I've never seen you so disheveled."

Banks rolled her eyes. "I know," she said. "I don't know what's wrong with me. I'm usually so prepared and organized, and now

I feel like I've been hit by a train. Particularly with the one case. It just feels like a sea full of questions that I have answers to, but they're worth almost nothing because there's no proof. And none of the answers I have are just shy of the mark for something to connect it all. It's just a whole lot of nothing!"

As Banks was having a very quiet meltdown to save from curiosity from her coworkers, Wild was looking at her with some concern and some faint amusement. He glanced out of the window next to him, and something out of Banks' view caught his eye. He squinted for a moment (Banks had been telling him he needed glasses, but he would not listen) then shifted back into his concern, now also looking surprised. He spoke with wide eyes to Banks, though he kept his focus out the window.

"Banks," he said, quiet and stern, "I think you and I should go outside for a smoke break now."

Banks had noticed Wild's concern but was too tired to be that worried herself. "You know I don't smoke, Wild."

"Well then," Wild said, standing up and already beginning to move toward the door, "why don't you keep me company while I do? Come on."

He walked with purpose toward the door as the other officers glanced with curiosity in his direction but did nothing else. Banks got up from her chair and nearly had to jog to keep up with him. As she did, she glanced for a moment back to the Sergeant's office to see that the door was closed. She was glad of this because she had a feeling this was something that desired no interference.

When the two detectives stepped out of the police station, that hunch had turned out to be correct. Once walking up the sidewalk and now stopped not five feet in front of them, was a thin, blonde-haired woman who looked to be in her mid-fifties. Her hair was done up in a glamorous and youthful style, and the only makeup that she seemed to wear was a bright red lipstick. She wore a red blouse and white knee-length skirt, giving her the impression of being a decent amount younger than she must have been. She removed a pair of white cat-eye sunglasses to reveal bright blue eyes, which stared at the two detectives. Wide-open and receptive, they and not nearly as shocked as the detectives' eyes were. And gladly, too, as this woman was the physical embodiment of hope for Banks, and that was no exaggeration.

"Oh, hello," the woman said, shifting into a kind smile. "I'm sorry, I came to speak with a Detective Banks?" She held her hand out. "My name is Violet McMullen."

09:52 AM.

Wild, ever the savior of the day, had made up an excuse to the Sergeant about going out to investigate so that he, Banks, and Mrs. McMullen could take a trip to Banks' apartment. Mrs. McMullen did not seem nearly as confused about this situation as either detective would have expected her to be.

Speaking of expectations, Mrs. McMullen herself was considerably different in person from the woman Banks had imagined her to be. Banks had always thought of her as the distraught woman from the stories. That woman was crying, hearing the news of her adopted daughter and her secret lover were both running away, and she would never see them again. She was the devastated widow telling her children that their father had been murdered. But the stylish lady who now sat across from Banks and Wild at Banks' small little dining table was a different person entirely. She was the picture of bliss, a snapshot out of a trendy catalog for women with their lives together. Her statement color choices and graceful mannerisms did not suggest any trauma or sadness.

The three of them sat at the aforementioned table, the sounds of city traffic outside and quiet radio playing in the background. They sipped coffee that Banks had made for them, each unsure who should speak first. If this were a routine interrogation, either of the detectives would begin with their ideally pre-prepared questions, for which they would receive answers from the civilian. But this was not routine, and Violet McMullen had come looking for *Banks*, not the other way around.

Mrs. McMullen made pleasantries, complimenting Banks' home and graciously smiling as they made proper introductions, now that they were in safe quarters and not standing in the middle of a Montgomery sidewalk, outside of a crowded Montgomery precinct.

After an awkward silence had gone on for long enough, Banks began her proceedings.

"Mrs. McMullen," she said, "I have a few things I would like to ask you about if you'll allow me."

"Of course, Detective," Mrs. McMullen responded, gracious as ever. "I had things I wished to inform you of."

"Well, then let's begin there," Banks said, feeling at ease for not being the instigator for once. "What did you wish to inform me of?"

Mrs. McMullen took a deep breath, not sighing for sorrow but rather preparing for what she must have felt was a rather significant moment. She set her coffee mug down on the table and put her hands in her lap as she launched herself back in time, as Banks had seen quite a few times now.

11:06 AM.

It had been just over an hour since Mrs. McMullen had begun her story, but you would never know based on the interest of the two detectives who sat across from her. Banks had been sitting with her hand over her mouth for the past half hour, and Wild sat like a statue, maintaining raised eyebrows.

When she finished what she had to say, Mrs. McMullen took another deep breath to imply her completion, and Banks looked to Wild as he looked back at her. Both of them had wide eyes.

Banks took her hand off of her mouth and took a breath to collect herself.

"Well, Mrs. McMullen," she said. "That certainly changes things."

Mrs. McMullen looked at the detective with upturned eyebrows, her expression a perfect mix of worry and hope.

"I hope you'll forgive me, keepin' it to myself for so long," she said. "It was for a good reason, you know. And even if I was volunteerin' it for everyone's ears, those detectives never wanted to hear nothin' from me. As years went on, I thought I should say somethin', but any time I tried to tell someone somethin', they just would not believe me that anythin' I had to say was worth the trouble."

Banks nodded, for she knew that situation well.

Mrs. McMullen continued. "Then, when Betty told me you were pokin' around about things, well... I was worried, you know. Not for any reason you'd think, though. I was mostly worried about my sanity, if I'm honest. I didn't know if I could dig this up again. But she told me that it was a woman investigatin', and, no offense detective..." She addressed Wild for her last point, and he showed no sign of any offense, so she continued to Banks. "I thought you might be the one to finally listen to me. And I thought that if you were gonna discover the truth, I wanted you to hear it from me."

Banks nodded again and quickly tried to order her thoughts into something coherent before pressing on. Her first instinct was to laugh, which she did a little, to her guests' surprise.

"I'm sorry," Banks said. "I just thought about when I spoke to El— Betty. When I spoke to Betty, and, if you'll forgive me, we actually wondered if you might've shot one of them. To protect someone or something like that, of course, neither of us suspected you were a cold-hearted killer."

Mrs. McMullen accepted Banks' past theory with a small smile and a shake of the head. "Yes, she mentioned that on the telephone. She just asked me, 'Mamma, you didn't kill anybody, did ya?' You should have seen my face. I told her I didn't, of course, but I didn't tell her the whole story because I figured if I came and told you, she'd know sooner or later.

"You know, there is one thing they never gave me the chance to say: when we were in the room together, Roger came for me first. Bet you didn't know that. He was ravin' drunk, and when he saw the two of us there, and we shot up an' all, he came and tried to hit me before he even tried for Tom. You should have seen the look in his eyes, but Tom wouldn't let him have me. He fought him off, and that was when he got punched the first time. He distracted the monster for long enough that he didn't want to deal with me anymore, and the two of them went out. I never saw Roger alive again, and don't think me indecent when I tell you that I don't regret it. He tormented me for long enough.

"That Tom," Mrs. McMullen continued with a softer tone. "You know, he's the reason I kept quiet for as long as I did. He never wanted me to tell a soul. I'll never forget the way he held my shoulders as they were goin' away, lookin' into my eyes. He said, 'you didn't see a thing, Violet, you hear me? It's real important that you don't tell anyone what you saw. I'm gonna take care of it, don't you worry.' Well, he sure did. But I'm tired of lettin' him play the martyr, Detective. I won't let it continue."

Banks and Wild looked at each other a moment, and Wild nudged Banks' arm, which was his unique, subtle way of congratulating her or pointing something out, or most other things. But Banks knew precisely what this one meant. Wild was saying, Look at that, you've finally got something.

"I know," she responded to his silent remark. She then looked back to Mrs. McMullen, who looked back at her expectantly.

"So, what'll you do now?" Mrs. McMullen asked her.

"Well," Banks said. "I think I'll have to make one last visit to Tom Higgins and tell him what I know. I think he might finally tell me the truth now."

~ 17 ~

THE WHOLE TRUTH AND
NOTHING BUT THE TRUTH

SATURDAY, SEPTEMBER 4, 1965. 08:03 AM.

Everything was familiar, except for the feeling in her chest.

As Isla Banks walked through the halls of Dothan penitentiary, for what she thought might be the last time, there was the feeling of comforting familiarity trying to get through and relax her, but the tension that remained would let nothing else in. She tried to be optimistic, but the weight of the confrontation she would have in mere minutes was enough to sink her into the ground.

Ripley, the guard, had been surprised to see her, and the office lady, who Banks finally learned was called Janice, sounded to have just about jumped out of her skin when Banks had called to set up a meeting. Banks supposed that she had not made much effort to cover how she felt when she left there previously.

Now, she strolled through with purpose. Ripley never said a word, but he did sneak a look back at her now and then, and she wondered what the gossip had been in her absence. But, however egotistically conscious she had been and typically was, she found no time for such trivial considerations at the present moment.

And there it is, Banks thought, as they reached the door to the same cell she had seen Tom in all the times before. She knew that he would be behind the door, and she also knew that he would be reluctant to talk since she had needed to force him to see her. She hated that he had made her do that, and now she was afraid of what he would say or not. She had tried too many times, in vain, to revert to "cold detective," but every time she had tried, she reminded herself that there was no use lying to herself to preserve herself from fear and anxiety because it would not work. Either way, the day would move along and then end, whether or not she permitted it.

Ripley went about the usual procedure and opened the door, but he did not go in first to cuff Tom this time. Instead, he let Banks enter and closed the door behind her, without anything more. Banks looked to the man sitting at the interrogation table and first noticed that he had not been cuffed earlier, either. His hands were free, and he laid them in his lap as he looked down at the table, avoiding her eye.

He was beginning to revert into the first version that Banks had seen when she first met him. He had dark circles around his eyes; he had not been sleeping well. His hair was still not as long as it had been before, but it was scraggly, as was the rest of him. He did not look at her until she sat down, and when she did, he glanced up and directly into her eyes. His eyes were red and shiny. He had been crying recently.

Banks felt awful for being there. She felt as though she was directly harming him by showing her face there. However, there was no real reason for her to feel this way, not now. After all, she could finally be confident that she was there for his benefit.

"Hello, Tom," she said.

Tom took a breath in, and Banks almost started crying herself when he smiled. The smile was not as carefree as it was supposed to be, but it was a smile, nonetheless.

"Hey there, Detective," he said in a gravelly, tired voice. "I don't look so good, do I?"

Banks returned his smile in an attempt to put him at some ease. She desperately wanted to help him, just as she had in her dreams.

"You've looked better," she said, trying to tease him in a friendly manner. "What have you been doing?"

Tom did not look surprised that she was showing interest. He seemed more open to conversation than he had the last time she had seen him, when he had called her a liar.

"Ain't been sleepin'," he said. "Been pickin' fights an' all. I forgot how to spend my time when you started visiting. For the past couple of months, I've spent most of my time thinkin' about the past."

"Was that a bad thing?" Banks asked.

Tom sighed. "No," he said. "No, I guess not."

A moment passed in silence, and Banks seized the opportunity to begin down her intended track. She reached in her briefcase bag and pulled out a tape recorder. She set up the recorder on the table with the microphone directed between them while he watched her. His expression didn't change; he just stared. When she finished setting up, she sat back up but did not press record yet. She had no intention of continuing unfairly. She wanted Tom to talk because *he* wanted to.

"I know you don't want to discuss this with me anymore, Tom," she said. "I know I lied to you, but it was because I knew you would keep the truth from me. I hoped that if it just felt like a casual conversation with nothing at stake, then you might be more likely to tell me what happened. I see how I betrayed your trust, and I'm sorry."

Tom looked directly into Banks' soul. She could almost see the ocean that he was trying to keep himself afloat in.

"You're an oddball, Detective," he said. "Apologizin' like that. Ain't nothin', I guess. But I already told you what I know. You might not have gotten what you wanted, but you got what I could give."

Banks had grown tired of being delicate. She put everything on the line.

"I know the truth, now, Tom," she said. "I *know* you didn't kill those men."

Tom gave her the same defiance he always did. Then, when Banks did not falter, his eyebrows came in slightly, and he seemed to realize that this was more than a bold claim. He said nothing and waited patiently for the rest of what Banks had prepared.

"And I also know why," she said. "I know why you said what you said. I know why you lied."

Tom took a moment to discern the seriosity of the accusation. Upon deciding its true urgency, he said certainly, "You talked to Violet."

"Yes, I did," Banks said, having promised not to lie. "She came to me, Tom, and she told me everything. Everything she knows, anyway. The rest I've pretty much worked out."

Banks waited a beat for Tom to say something, but he remained in his silence, watching her as she gave everything she had left to give.

"Violet never saw any gun when you went down to the barn with her husband," she said, suddenly finding ease in her tone after feeling a burst of adrenaline. "Because you didn't have one. You never even grabbed one from your house. But when she saw you come out of the barn, when she saw the *two of you* come out of the barn..."

As she said that, Tom let out a sharp breath, the beginnings of a sob. Banks took a moment's pause, and the two of them looked at each other. Tom pleaded with her without speaking, but Banks could not oblige.

"You told me I was lying, Tom, and I'm very sorry," she said. "But you lied to me first. You told me Diamond McMullen was not present at the crime scene that night."

"*Please,*" Tom begged quietly, though seemingly as loud as he could muster.

"Tom," Banks said, softer than she was speaking previously, "I'm sorry, but I can't stop. Because it was a lie. She was there that night, and that isn't all."

She purposefully paused there, wanting to change course before continuing with the *real* story. Tom just sat there, and a single tear fell from his eye and down his cheek.

"I remembered what you said," she said. "That if I had been paying attention, I would have known what kind of man you are. I don't know if you meant to say that, but you were right, and I *do* know. You are the kind of man who looks out for people. You protect people who cannot look out for themselves. You are kind and compassionate, and that has never once changed. You would give anything to protect your friends, right?"

Tom blinked. Something had changed in his expression. He was not crumbling so much as he had been before.

"If you know so much," he said, more evenly than before, "then what the hell do you need from me?"

Banks lent forward and folded her hands on the table. "I need you to remember that man. You've kept him locked up in a cage for so long, but I can see him through the cracks. It's not the man they think you are, not who they locked up in this prison, not even who you see in the mirror. You let him out for just a brief moment when you were forced to face your past. Then you threw him back in his cage. I'm asking you to let him go.

"I want you to tell me the truth about that night. I *need* you to tell me; you are the only person who can. You know everything that I need to get you out of here. I know you don't think you deserve it. You're punishing yourself by sacrificing your freedom, but it's not right. You don't deserve to be in here, Tom; please help me. I can't get you out of here alone."

Tom held his ground as she spoke, but he looked split in two. One half of his being was listening to her, straining to help, but the other half was keeping the first behind iron bars. Seeing that she was breaking through, Banks continued to her main point.

"They never found her, you know," Banks said, finding more solid ground with every step. "They didn't spend a lot of time looking. You knew they wouldn't, and you were right. They searched again after they found the gun, and they came up with nothing. She could be anywhere by now or nowhere. I can promise you that they won't if you don't want them to. If she's alive out there, she is safe from this, just like you wanted. You've served your purpose in here, and now it's time to see the sun again."

Tom took another shaky breath but spoke with a solid tone.

"I can't," he said. "I can't face them again. Even if they know the truth, I don't know if I can go back. It hurts too much."

Tom looked into her eyes, and Bank looked into his. He had finally admitted that there was more to the truth. Banks tried to access something that would act as a turning point, which he needed to surrender fully.

Then it hit her.

"Isla," she almost blurted, her mouth moving too fast for her mind again. Tom furrowed his brows slightly, confused by the seemingly unrelated comment. "My first name, it's Isla. I never told you my first name because I wanted to avoid a personal connection, but I am far past that now. I don't want to embarrass myself, but you need to know that I care a hell of a lot for you, Tom Higgins. Because even if you don't want to let that part of you go, I've fallen in love with him. And I'm not the only one. All the people you think you've hurt, even if you did, care for you because they know how you cared for them. You are loved and forgiven.

"But regardless of that personal connection, I'm a Detective, Tom. I put up with a lot to be here doing what I am doing, and I do it so the innocent can walk freely in this country that I love/I'm not asking you anymore, Tom. Help me get you out of here, so that innocent man in you can be free, and the people who love you can show you themselves just how much."

It was silent in the cell. The moment lasted long enough that Banks thought her plea had failed. But after more than a minute of sitting there, Tom smiled again.

"It's nice to meet you, Isla," he said. "I guess I have my orders. I'm scared as shit, I'll be honest, but I guess it's time."

Banks sighed louder than she had intended and realized how much breath she had been holding. She looked into Tom's eyes as she pressed 'record.'

"This is Detective Isla Banks, interrogating Thomas Higgins, aged twenty-seven—"

Tom waved at her so she would stop, not wanting to interrupt on tape. When he had her attention, he silently held up eight fingers. Of course, Banks thought. She was so wrapped up in everything, she had forgotten that Tom's birthday had passed. She nodded to him and almost went to start speaking again, but then another idea sprung to mind, and she rewound the tape to begin the recording again.

"This is Detective Isla Banks, interrogating Thomas *Peter* Higgins, aged twenty-eight. The date is September fourth, nineteen sixty-five, presenting new testimony on the case of murder on Roger McMullen and Alan Tucker Holt on September twenty-first, nineteen fifty-five..."

* * *

I guess the first thing that needs clearin' up is the order. Mr. Mc-Mullen wasn't shot first. It was Tuck.

Tuck had been waitin' around the house tryin' to get me in trouble. He had heard what I'd been up to with Mrs., and he was figurin' he would get me sent down the road. Now, no one ever told me that was why, but Kitch had told me one day that word had gone out through the boys about the affair, even though it wasn't supposed to, and now ol' Tuck knew about it. I had been thinkin' it was odd that he hadn't said anything about it, but I can't think of another reason why he would have been around the house so late that night, 'course I can't ask him now. They all thought I was dead, but maybe he'd figured out that it was a lie. Either way, he was around there when we went out to the barn.

You know the lead-up and all. Mr. McMullen took me on out there and started beatin' me. I tried to fight him off, but he had a drunken fury, and he caught me off guard. I didn't think he'd be so strong.

Now, this is where it's different. I didn't have a gun with me; you're right. It killed me to leave all of 'em behind because of my daddy. But I figured if they sent the dogs after us for Miss Diamond runnin' away, I wouldn't get in as much trouble without a gun on me. I wonder what woulda happened if I did have one.

So I was pretty helpless that night, I can't lie. I figured I was gonna die right there. After fightin' for a little, I gave up. I was just about slippin' away when someone else came in there and started wrestlin' Mr. McMullen offa me. It was Tuck, wouldn't you believe it. You already know he was a fighter, and he came in and saw I was gettin' killed, so he fought the old man off of me and got me on my feet.

He helped me over to the door, and we was just about out when I saw Miss Diamond comin' down the steps. She had her little bag and everything. She was ready to run.

Just after I saw her, we heard Mr. McMullen yellin' behind us. We turned around and saw him there, pointin' a gun at us. I s'pose he had it the whole time, and if he didn't beat me to death, he woulda shot me for what I'd been doin'. I hate to think what woulda happened to Violet after that.

He had the gun up, and we was shoutin' back, tryin' to get him to calm down, but he was seein' red, you know. He aimed for me and pulled the trigger, but Tuck was already movin', and he pushed me out of the way. The bullet caught Tuck in the gut, and he was gone 'fore I could do anything about it.

Now, I didn't look back for Miss Diamond because I was too afraid. When Tuck fell, Mr. McMullen realized he'd hit the wrong sumbitch. He paused for a second, but he was too drunk to care and got ready to shoot me, too. I woulda ran, but I was still beat up good, bleedin' an' all. Even if I walked, I was limpin', and I knew that if I tried to get away, Miss Diamond would be with me, and he mighta missed again and shot her. Now, you know I couldn't let that happen.

So I just stood there with my hands up, beggin' him to leave me be and have some mercy. He hesitated, and I think it was 'cause he'd already shot someone, and it was settin' in what he'd done. But he knew he could have gotten away with it. He had connections all over, and we were just some bastard kids.

I pleaded for my life. I've never been so helpless. The last thing I thought before it happened, as I closed my eyes and waited for him to shoot me, was I hoped to God that Miss Diamond wasn't watchin'.

Then I heard a shot, but I didn't feel anything. I opened my eyes, expectin' to see Mr. McMullen pointin' his gun, or a white light or somethin'. But when I opened my eyes, I was lookin' into the barn, and Mr. McMullen was on the ground bleedin', shot dead.

Then I heard a little voice behind me, and I knew what had happened.

She said, "I'm sorry, Tom. I know you told me not to do nothin'."

I turned around and looked at Miss Diamond standin' there, scared in the face, holdin' my revolver in her only hand.

***

08:37AM.

"Where did Diamond get the gun?" Banks asked, mind spinning, but less like a car wreck and more like a record. "And how did she know how to shoot?"

Tom sighed, though now he didn't look as resigned as he had before. He seemed almost relieved.

"She stole it from me," he said. "Best thing about a double-action revolver is you don't need to cock it yourself. All you gotta do is pull the trigger. It works real good for someone with one hand, apparently. And as for *how*, that was another time I didn't tell you everything. I told you before that I didn't let her shoot it when we was at my house that one time. But I *did* let her shoot it just once. I didn't see the harm since no one would know. She got a little kickback the first time, but she was ready for it that night."

Banks nodded, not surprised by anything at this point, regardless of this very new information. She was only just getting started.

"And what about the other gun?" She asked. "Mr. McMullen's gun."

"We took it," Tom responded, allowing a sly smile. "Well, I took it, technically, with good reason. The whole gun situation was tricky. Before we took the VM, Miss Diamond thought we should place my gun in Tuck's hand, but by then, I'd taken it from *her* before I realized there would be my fresh fingerprints on it if I did. Not my best judgment, I admit it. Plus, we'd had our differences, but ol' Tuck saved my life, you know. I didn't want to make him look like a killer after that, even if he wasn't there to see it. I ain't a monster.

"The other thing you gotta realize is this: Miss Diamond didn't know this, but even before we left, I already knew I wasn't gonna make it very far, not in my state. And I came to the quick realization that someone was gonna have to fall for this. Especially with all the people Mr. McMullen knew who'd be lookin' for someone to blame, maybe they'd even think Violet did it. Still, since most people thought I was dead, we tried to run for it. We kept my gun because of the fingerprints, and we took McMullen's Victory Model for protection, so we could both have one because I was pretty sure we were gonna have to go our separate ways."

"So the Victory Model wasn't yours?" Banks asked.

"Naw," he said. "I had a Smith and Wesson from my daddy, alright, but no model ten. Ol' McMullen fought in the war like my daddy did, and he stole the gun when he left the service. I s'pose the war was what made him drink so much, you know. But my daddy never came back from the war, and no one was gonna steal a dead man's gun and give it to his eight-year-old son. They woulda took it off him when he went down, and someone else woulda used it." Tom smirked at her. "Now, *that* lie I was sure you was gonna see-through."

Banks felt mildly annoyed at herself that she had let that detail go. She then became incredibly conscious of the recorder on the table and hoped they would let that slip in her logic go. She both loved *and* loathed the way Tom made her forget her common sense.

"So, what did you do then?" She asked.

"Well, we tried to get away. Violet found us comin' out, and I told her not to tell no one she saw us goin'. And she didn't; she didn't have to. They found me a little down the road, but we both said Diamond had run away, and we hadn't seen her at all."

"Why wasn't Diamond with you when you were found?" Banks asked, knowing the answer but asking for the sake of the tape.

"I told her to go on," he said. "I said I was gonna try and hide, and maybe, if Mrs. McMullen kept her word and they didn't find me, they would just think I was dead and wouldn't spend too long lookin' for me. I'd told Miss Diamond just to keep goin', and if I didn't get found, I'd catch up to her, even though I knew I probably wouldn't make it. She got a head start, and they were satisfied when they found me."

"You let them believe you did it on your own," Banks recounted. "So they wouldn't suspect Diamond had been involved."

Tom nodded. "Yeah, and I guess you could say I assisted her, but she only did what she did to protect me, like I'd tried doin' for her. I knew if they found out what Miss Diamond did, she'd end up in an institution or something, just another place where nobody cared about her. She woulda told 'em what she did, and you can be sure of that. She'd rat herself out to save me because she knew I'd do it for her. I couldn't bear the thought of that. She'd suffered enough.

"It was hell tryin' to get her to leave me, though. She wanted to stay behind, but I got all stern and said, 'Miss Diamond, now you know I'm a gentleman, and if I'm gonna get found, I want it to be on my terms. I'm never gonna let them get you, not if my life depends on it. You've been kept back for too long, now let me do this my way.' And she started cryin', don't you know it? I can see her little face in my mind. I wonder if she's still waitin' for me to catch up."

Banks made a closing remark for that segment of the interview to emphasize the point of the conversation, why they were there in the first place.

"Just to reiterate, Tom," she said, "you didn't kill anyone, correct?"

"No, ma'am." Tom smiled just for her to see. "I never killed a soul."

"You took the blame to save your friend," she said, never breaking their eye contact.

"Yes, ma'am," he said, strong and sure. "I took the blame so she could be free."

~ 18 ~

INTO THE LION'S DEN

Isla Banks and Tom Higgins sat in the clear air that now inhabited the interrogation room. The purpose was now complete, but Banks had more questions to ask. She felt confident that this was, finally, the whole truth. And the truth is always easier to prove than fabrications. She took a deep breath and continued with the technicalities.

"So," she said. "What happened with the guns after that? You didn't keep one behind with you, so she took both of them?"

"When I knew I was stayin' behind," Tom said. "I took another bullet out of the victory model so it would look like that was the only gun used. I had her take both and the bullet and told her to throw away the Victory Model so she wouldn't be found with it, but to hide it far away, so she'd be long gone by the time they found it. Then I told her to throw the bullet away somewhere different, so if one of them was found, they wouldn't find 'em together."

Banks closed her eyes for a second and felt a soothing wave of recognition come over her. She reached into the front pocket of her bag and pulled out the bullet from the creek. She had been keeping it with her, believing in its significance but not certain about where it fit. She held it out to Tom, and he took it, warm hands brushing hers before he acquired the bullet.

"I have here a bullet that I found in the woods near a creek we've spoken of previously in these sessions, Mr. Higgins," she said, speaking clearly for the tape. "Is that the same bullet?" She asked, hoping she knew the answer.

Tom smiled at the small piece of metal, examining it. "It sure is, detective," he said. "I can't believe it, but that's the same one, no question."

He set the bullet down horizontally on the table between them.

"Fortunately them guns are similar enough that the ammunition is the same," he continued his retelling, "They's both thirty-eights, and both Smith and Wesson. It was like fate. I figured at the time that if they thought it was just the one gun used, even if they found it somewhere, they wouldn't know she had another gun with her. That was so she could protect herself but also to have somethin' to remember me by in case I didn't make it, but I didn't say that to her."

"But why did you say the model ten was your gun?" Banks asked.

"Well," Tom sighed again. "That was just to make things look a little better. By then, they were askin' about Diamond, and I was all nervous, you know. But they'd pretty much decided that I'd done it no matter what I said, and it looks better if I shot the man with my gun and not his. Just a pride thing, really, a little dignity. I was hopin' for some points from someone since the lawyer wasn't gonna give me none."

"The state lawyer, Matthews, you mean?" Banks asked, eyes flitting from Tom to the recorder and back again. She was less surprised at this remark than she would have liked to be, as she had been somewhat disappointed at the attorney's approach in the court transcript. While she needed no convincing, this conversation was about the tape and subsequently the jury.

"That's the one," Tom confirmed, rolling his eyes at the memory.

"Why do you mention him, Tom?" She asked him.

Tom smiled, knowing the significance of what he had said, and leaning gleefully into the drama of the accusation, ever a natural showman. "At the time, I thought it was just because of the situation. A law-abiding man and a criminal hooligan, it wasn't like we was gonna be friends, and I knew that. But that ain't the whole story. I heard tell of it when I was in my third year here. Somebody said ol' Matthews got tipped off, bribed by somebody who fought with Mr. McMullen in the war, told him to put me under, no questions asked. He's a cop, too, and word is he'd done it more than once. The fella who told me about it ended up getting out of here early, bless him, but that cop tried to put him under, too."

Banks raised her eyebrows. Corruption in law enforcement was not unheard of, and this revelation could be another turning point when the trial returned to court. She put her pen to her notebook, ready to write.

"Do you know what the cop's name was?" She asked. "The one who bribed the lawyer?"

As prepared to write as she was, she was unknowingly unprepared for the answer.

"They said his name was Walter Nichols," Tom said. "You might know him. I hear he's a sergeant up in Montgomery, now."

MONDAY, SEPTEMBER 13, 1965. 07:59 AM.

The sound of Banks' shoes on linoleum was a symphony, and regardless of her bodily exhaustion, she found she could not have been more awake and focused that morning. Aflush with purpose and hope, she marched through the station reception and into the bullpen. This was not only the feeling she lived for as a detective and had experienced at least a few times; this was especially satisfying. If the previous battles of her mind were the likes of Bunker Hill, she was now in Yorktown.

The revelation of Sgt. Nichols' involvement in Tom's trial made everything crystal clear. His reluctance to let Banks have the case, his vigorous opposition to its continuance, and anger when Banks pressed him. Everything made sense now, and not only that; if Banks had not been determined to finish the case before, now she would die to see it done.

"He can rot in that cell forever for all I care because he's guilty! What is the point of diggin' into this anymore, Detective?"

Banks smirked as she made eye contact with Wild, who got up from his desk and joined her parade. The two of them had been hard at work for the past week, making visits and organizing evidence for Tom's case as well as their everyday work. Wild had even reluctantly agreed to meet with Banks the previous evening to prepare for the morning events. Wild seemed to be more visibly tired than Banks was, but he nevertheless stayed by her side as they marched toward Sgt. Nichols' office.

They stood outside the open door, waiting politely for admission. The Sergeant looked up from his coffee as he read the newspaper, saw them standing there, and waved them in reluctantly. He put his coffee mug down but continued to read.

"What can I do for y'all?" He asked them, keeping his gaze in his paper.

Wild and Banks looked at each other, and Wild nodded. Banks smiled and took a deep breath before speaking.

"We've got something new," she said, "on the Higgins case."

On the word, 'Higgins,' the Sergeant shot his wide eyes up at them, and he began to redden immediately. Realizing the extremity of his reaction, he cleared his throat and looked back down to his paper in an attempt to hide his feelings.

"I thought I told you to drop that, Detective," he said to his paper, successfully maintaining a smooth tone but giving off incriminating energy that everyone in the bullpen must have felt.

"You did, sir—" Banks began.

"Well," Sgt. Nichols interrupted before she could get anything else out, looking back up and smiling evilly, "then that's it, ain't it?"

"Except that it isn't," Wild said, and the Sergeant looked to him with furrowed eyebrows.

Sgt. Nichols rolled his eyes and sighed, folding up his newspaper and taking off his reading glasses. "And what do you mean by that, now?"

Wild looked to Banks, who gratefully took the lead back from him. Wild was there for support and security, but this was Banks' victory.

"What we mean is this," she said, leaning forward to set the case folder gently on the Sergeant's desk. "Have a look."

The Sergeant sighed again and opened the folder. He looked at it for about three seconds before getting impatient. "What am I looking at, Detective?"

"Evidence," Banks said. "Evidence that proves Tom Higgins is not guilty of murdering Roger McMullen or Alan Tucker Holt."

The Sergeant looked warily up at her before rifling through the first few files. He came across some crime-scene pictures, and before he could ask their significance, Banks jumped in to explain.

"The blood splatters coming from the bodies," she began, "they didn't try to examine them last time because that method was in its very beginning in '55. Upon returning to those photos from the crime scene, I had the forensic lab look into the formation of the splatters. They confirmed that while Alan Holt *was* shot from the front, The bullet through Roger McMullen's head must have come from the front and not the back, because it splattered in the opposite direction. It looked like he had been shot from behind because he fell forward, but he was not. It's so obvious when you look at it; I can't believe they missed it."

The Sergeant was silent as he moved papers. Banks continued her excited explanation without apparent malice because she had already decided to save the biggest point for the very end.

"As for the weapons," Banks continued, "The Victory Model was not Higgins', it was McMullen's. His wife and daughters found the paperwork for it to prove his ownership. McMullen had a local gunman fabricate the paperwork because it was stolen property. Mc-Mullen stole it when he was in the service, but the serial number and everything else match the weapon. Not only that, but Higgins' gun papers, which we had the entire time, do not match the weapon in question but rather list a different model of Smith and Wesson revolver. The kicker is that the serial number and the title of "Model Ten" had been manually recorded on the copies included in the file, whereas the originals, which were, until a few days ago, stored in a separate location, listed the correct serial number for that model. The brand and serial number were enough to convince the jury, which was the intention because it is clear someone tampered with the records."

The Sergeant was on to the game now but needed not to reveal anything in his expression. The sweat on his forehead was enough.

"And there, behind them," she said, pointing, "is the new transcript from a tape, recorded while I had a conversation with Higgins recently, in which he describes the entire scene. His testimony matches these details exactly."

The Sergeant looked about to speak, likely to discount the worth of a criminal's testimony. Just then, Banks heard footsteps from the other side of the office door and knew it was time to go in for the kill.

"Not so fast, Sarge," she said, holding up a finger and resisting the urge to smile. "Because there's more. Remember I said the originals to Higgins' gun records were stored in a separate location. The location in question was the home office of Mr. Conrad Matthews, esquire, the prosecuting attorney for the Higgins trial, the man who got him locked up. I paid him a visit upon Higgins' suggestion, and he was very ready and willing to give me the whole story." Banks put her hands on Nichol's desk, leaning in to look in the Sergeant's eye. "I guess some people don't want to live with their sins forever, particularly when there's someone else who needs to pay the penance for it."

The Sergeant stood his ground while simultaneously unaware that he was playing directly into Banks' hands.

"I don't know what you're suggesting, Detective," he said, raising his voice just a little, and Banks saw Wild step just a little forward out of the corner of her eye. "Or what you think you're accomplishing here, but if it worked before, it'll work again. I could get you in serious trouble for working this case against direct orders. You're treading dangerous territory, doll."

"Oh, Walter, I wouldn't say that, now," A voice boomed from behind them.

Banks smiled in the Sergeant's face before standing up straight and moving to the side to allow the new person to come forward. The two detectives nodded in respect to Captain Roy Johnston, a man about the same age as the Sergeant, but nearly a foot taller. The Captain ducked under the door frame and strolled into the office with a relaxed expression, walking with a wooden cane but maintaining a powerful presence.

Upon learning of Sgt. Nichols' involvement with the case and his obstruction, Banks had gone immediately to the Captain, albeit with some concern. The concern in question dissipated when the Captain informed her that he had no knowledge of the pulled case in the first place because the Sergeant had done it by his own accord. Upon speaking to Banks and Wild about the new evidence and turning tides of the Higgins case, the Captain agreed that the Sergeant should be held accountable. Thus, he planned this appearance in the office now with them to confront the now red-in-the-face Sergeant, who stood straight as his superior entered.

"Captain," he said, nodding with respect but looking shocked.

The Captain nodded to Banks and Wild before addressing the Sergeant. "Walter, you've really done it now, son," he said. "I go on office leave for a little while, and all your skeletons are fallin' willy-nilly out of the closet, old boy."

The Sergeant was very clearly perturbed by being called both 'son' and 'old boy.' He tried to keep himself together as he defended his actions.

"Sir," he said, and Banks got a curious amount of enjoyment at the Sergeant needing to formally address someone, "Surely you don't think this whole situation is really as serious as Detective Banks is making it, do you? After all, this was ten years ago."

"It sure has, Sergeant," Captain Johnston said. "Ten years you've let an innocent man rot in a cell. That's exactly the opposite of your job, correct?"

The Sergeant held in a small breath. "Yes, sir," he said through nearly gritted teeth.

"And not only that," the Captain said, gesturing to Banks and Wild, "but I would think this applies to obstruction of justice, wouldn't you think so, Detectives?" Both detectives nodded in affirmation, and the Captain looked back to the Sergeant. "So I would think that would result in your arrest, Walter."

The Sergeant turned red as a tomato as Wild went around his desk to arrest him. As he cuffed him and read his rights, Wild winked at Banks, who stood there with Captain Johnston, resisting the urge to smile.

The Sergeant said nothing while Wild escorted him out of the office and to a holding cell. Captain Johnston and Banks lingered behind, witnessing the other officers in the bullpen watching in awe as Wild took the detained Sergeant away. The Captain nudged Banks' arm with his cane.

"You're allowed to look a little happy, Detective," he said, smiling a little himself.

"That's not what it's about, Captain," Banks said. "This isn't personal; it's just the job."

"That's true," Captain Johnston said, "but celebrating little victories is how you get through the mess of it. You did good work, Detective. You know, maybe you'll take that job, someday. A *female* Sergeant, how about that!"

Banks furrowed her brow a little as the Captain nudged her again, smiling genuinely at her before returning to his own office. She knew that he meant what he said, however misguided the latter point had been. After all, there *had* been female sergeants before. Banks sighed and smiled a little.

Little victories, she thought.

8:43 PM.

Wild and Banks were back at Easy's that night, and this time Banks was in much better spirits. Now, *this* was what going to Easy's was supposed to feel like: a well-deserved celebration at a volume suitable to Wild's stern demeanor.

"You did good, Banks," Wild said between sips of his old fashioned.

"We both did," she said. "I'm glad you convinced me to give it another shot."

"That's what partners are for," he said. "We make a good team, kid."

Banks smiled at Wild's emotional indulgence. "Wild, I think you need to slow down on the old fashioned's."

Wild furrowed his brow and looked down at his half-empty drink. "What makes you say that?"

"Compliments *and* you called me, 'kid?' If you don't stop soon, you might make a whole facial expression for once."

Wild rolled his eyes and took another sip before making a wide and unnatural toothy smile that made Banks snort and cover her face.

"Okay," she said. "Never do that again."

Wild chuckled a little himself. "Well, you know I feel like I owe you a little compassion. As much as I say I trust you, I didn't fight nearly enough to help you with that case. I let him send you out on your own, and I'm sorry."

Banks rolled her own eyes. "Oh, Wild, it's not your fault," she said. "But while we're being honest, I should have asked you for help earlier than I did. I'm a newbie still, and I have thoughts that go a million miles a minute. If there's one thing I learned from this experience, it's that sometimes a more careful and patient approach might be better."

Wild nodded, and the two of them continued their drink, both of them eagerly looking forward to a long and prosperous partnership.

~ 19 ~

CLOSING TIME

TUESDAY, SEPTEMBER 21, 1965. 1:16 PM.

The humidity did its best to subdue the easy breath that flowed into Detective Isla Banks' lungs, but it did not stand a chance against the importance of the day. After a two-day trial ending on the ten-year anniversary of the crime, Detective Banks accompanied Tom Higgins out of the courthouse, relishing in his regained freedom.

The jury had not been as immediate in their decision to free Tom as another had been to put him in jail. Banks could not help but feel the plummeted irony of this fact. They had carefully considered the facts as the state attorney had called his witnesses. These witnesses included Tom himself, Conrad Matthews, and even Violet McMullen herself had spoken on the stand. Banks was relieved to see that people had been listening respectfully as Mrs. McMullen spoke after she had practically begged the woman to testify. And As Tom and Isla walked down the courthouse steps, Violet came to meet them.

"Hey there, Tom," she said, smiling at the young man.

Tom smiled back at her. "Thank you, Mrs. You know that meant the world to me."

"It's the least I could do," she said. "And thank you, Detective."

"I didn't do a thing but steer," Banks said.

The three of them stood for a moment in silence, and then another came to join them.

"Well, my eyes must be deceivin' me," Tom said to the newcomer. "That can't be Miss Betty."

Eliza Miller, who had traveled from Enterprise to attend the trial, smiled meekly at Tom. "It sure is, Tom," she said, mildly uncomfortable but speaking against her comfort level for the good of her mind. "For better or worse."

"Well, it sure is nice to see ya," Tom said. "I hear the detective here paid you a visit. I sure am glad you came."

It was then that Banks and Violet stepped away with an excuse of a needed conversation. They let Tom and Eliza speak privately, both of them agreeing that both parties should have that closure. After a few minutes of pretending not to be watching, the conversation ended, and Eliza and her mother said their goodbyes, leaving Banks and Tom to continue walking away from the courthouse and toward Banks' Bel Air.

"Boy, ain't life somethin' else?" Tom said as they walked. "Took a long time, but I finally got to apologize."

"Well, it's never too late," Banks said.

"S'pose not," Tom said.

The two of them reached Banks' car, and after some hesitation, Tom got in the passenger seat. He looked a little uncomfortable, and Banks wondered if the man had ever gotten into a car by his own accord before. They sat in the Bel Air as Banks started it up and turned to her company.

"Now that you're officially out," she said. "I got you a little something."

Tom looked at her suspiciously as she reached into her briefcase bag and pulled out a present, flat and thin and wrapped in yellow paper. She handed it to him, and he took it gently, surprised by the gesture.

"Well, now Isla," he said, and Banks glowed at his use of her first name, "You know I feel bad 'cause I didn't get you nothin'."

"Just open it," she said.

Tom tore the paper open to reveal the back of a record sleeve. He turned it around to read the record title: *Beatles for Sale.*

"It's your bug band!" He exclaimed while the both of them laughed. "Now I can see what the fuss is about."

"And it's the record with my favorite song on it," Banks said.

Tom smiled at the record as he searched the song list. "There it is, right?" He asked. "'I'll Follow the Sun.' That's it, ain't it?"

"Sure is."

It was silent except for Tom's subdued laughter as he looked at his new record. Then he looked up at Banks.

"You know," he said. "It's a good thing you got this for me because I don't know how I woulda bought it if you hadn't."

She could see the pensiveness in his face, and she knew he was wondering what he was going to do now that he had to make a living again.

"You know," Banks said, "I'm sure your old buddy Johnnie would give you a job. I'm sure he's dyin' to see you."

Tom smiled at her. "And what about you, Isla?" He asked. "You're not gonna go disappearin' on me now, are ya?"

Banks smiled back at him and put a hand on his cheek. "I wouldn't," she said."

3:22 PM.

Tom had wanted to see his home for years, and Banks was happy to grant that wish for him.

After the familiar trek to Dothan from the supreme court in Montgomery, Banks once again pulled her Bel Air in front of Tom's wooded homestead. She snuck a glance at Tom as she did so. There was youthful innocence in his eyes as he stared into his past, mentally preparing himself to walk into it again.

The two got out of the car and stepped gingerly toward the front door, which they soon discovered was still unlocked. As Tom turned the knob and took his first step in, something occurred to Banks, and she tried to get him to stop, but it was too late.

"Tom, wait—"

"Oh, those rat bastards," Tom whispered. He stood motionless and stared into the room at the back wall, where quite a few things were missing. "They took 'em all."

"I'm sorry," Banks said, stepping in behind him. "I should have told you."

He sighed. "It's nothin'," he said. "I figured they might be gone when I came back. Wait." Then he put a hand back to caution Banks not to move. He looked back at her quickly and mouthed: *I heard someone.* He then turned back around to keep a lookout.

Banks reached for her sidearm, which she thankfully had this time, to ready herself for whoever was lurking around. But before she could do more than touch it, she heard a step outside the open door behind her.

"Don't move," a voice said.

Tom had heard it, too. Neither of them moved a muscle, and Banks put her hands up. There had been no click, but Banks had the feeling there was a weapon pointed at her back.

"Montgomery police," she said. "We don't mean any harm. If I keep my hands up, will you allow me to turn around?"

The person did not respond, and Banks took a chance to slowly turn around, making small steps around, hands up all the time.

When she had turned fully, the first thing she recognized was there was, indeed, a gun pointed at her, by a person standing on the ground outside and down the front steps. Banks then looked further up the extended arm at the person holding it, the *woman*—

"You're trespassin'," the young woman said, and Banks found herself speechless, staring motionless.

"You listen here!" Tom said, still facing the other way. "This here is *my* house; you're the one who's trespassin'!"

"Oh my God," Banks managed as there was a tear forming in her eye. "You—"

"The owner of this house don't live here no more," the woman said, keeping her aim. "This is the last warning. Now, clear out."

"Tom," Banks croaked, and the woman furrowed her brow.

"What?" Tom responded, sounding increasingly irritated at this intrusion.

The woman's face went slack as long lost recognition came across her, and she lowered her aim with her only arm.

"Tom?" She asked in a much softer tone than she had previously had. Banks put her hands down slowly and shifted herself out of the way, turning just in time to see Tom turn around and look. Banks watched as tears immediately sprung to his shocked face, and she was feeling a few of her own as she witnessed the reunion in front of her.

"Tom Higgins?" she asked again, making a single, hesitant step forward as she squinted looking into the house. The petite young woman was much less intimidating now as she set her firearm on the ground. She wore a yellow shirt and dirt-covered overalls that were a couple of sizes too big for her thin frame, with similarly dirty shoes that were well past their day. Only one of her sleeves had an arm emerging from it. Her dark hair was a curly mess, and her light eyes shone with remembrance at the sight of her old friend.

"Oh my Lord," Tom said, his tone wobbling. "Well, ain't that somethin'?"

Tom touched Banks' shoulder as he passed her to walk out of the house and down the front steps to pull the girl into an embrace. She wrapped her arm around him, and they both began to cry. Banks put a hand to her mouth to keep her own sobs contained.

"Oh, my friend," Tom said into Diamond's shoulder, sniffing with emotion. "I'm sorry I left you all alone. But I ain't gonna do that no more, y'hear me?"

Diamond's tear-covered face was visible over Tom's shoulder, and Banks could see her open her eyes wide before pulling away.

"Tom, they took 'em," she said, tears still falling from her eyes as Tom held her shoulders. "Tom, they took your daddy's collection. I'm sorry, I was gone too long, and they took 'em away."

Tom laughed, his teary face beaming. He brought Diamond back into an embrace.

"I don't need 'em," he said. "I got all I need now."

EPILOGUE

* * *

The Sun is setting on the horizon. The ocean glitters in the afternoon light, peaceful and full of life. There is a boat floating out to sea, and she is in it. She does not row, but the vessel moves on its own, smoothly drifting away from shore. She knows how she got there. She is floating but not lost. She is looking for someone.

As she drifts further and further out, the sunset becomes moonlight, and she can no longer see the shore behind her, though she knows it is there. Something in the water becomes visible, floating at the surface. She wills the boat to approach it. As she comes closer, she can see a person working hard to keep their head above water. She knows him well.

She comes even closer and attempts, as she has before, to call out to him. This time, he hears her call, and he looks up to her, pleading, before he looks back down at the water just below his chin, panting as he keeps himself from drowning.

She knows what is below the surface, and she knows exactly what to do. She does not think about how deep the ocean is. She does not care. She dives over the side of her boat and into the murky depths. Swimming ever lower, she searches for what has been lost.

When she is so deep that she can no longer see the moonlight above, there is a soft green glow at the bottom. She knows that this is where the lost item is and that the item is not an item but a person. Pushing onward, she eventually makes out the shape of a child in the dim glow. Seeing that the child is alone at the bottom of the ocean, she pushes even harder to reach them. The child has grown since the last time she has seen her, and this time, she wears overalls, and her long, dark hair hangs suspended in the water around her, and her complexion is pale and ghostly. The woman knows the child's face like she would an old friend. The child's eyes are closed, and her mouth hangs open, unconscious. She has been down here for a long time.

Before the woman can grab the child's only arm, the child opens her eyes, but she is not drowning this time. She looks directly into the woman's own eyes and smiles. The child grabs the woman's arm and kicks off of the bottom of the ocean, carrying her along.

As they travel upward, the two great white sharks swim in a circle above them. The woman points at them, but the child continues to swim upward. They are traveling faster than ever before.

As the woman lets the child pull her, she sees that the child is not afraid of the ocean anymore. As they approach the surface, they can see him swimming at the surface. The woman kicks, swimming with the child, as neither looks back down at the sharks they know are under them.

They breach through to the surface, reuniting with the man. The three of them manage to board the woman's boat. They see the fins of the two sharks swimming away from them as they float back to shore...

* * *

Isla Banks opened her eyes into darkness, forgetting for a moment where she was. She sat up, looking around as a dim light was just beginning to peek through the window. Recognition fills her as she finds herself in the bedroom of Tom's house in Dothan. As her eyes began to adjust to the early morning dark, she looked up from the floor to where Tom was on the bed, softly snoring. The girl from her dream lay next to her on the floor, facing away but seemingly fast asleep.

Banks smiled and laid herself back down to go back to sleep. Just as she closed her eyes, she heard Diamond rollover just before feeling a poke on her arm.

Banks opened her eyes again and turned her head to face the girl, whose glowing blue eyes she could just make out in the dark.

"Thank you," the girl whispered.

Banks blinked and smiled as her contentment returned her to a sleepy state.

"Thank *you*," she replied.

CPSIA information can be obtained
at www.ICGtesting.com
Printed in the USA
BVHW082227180521
607644BV00010B/535

9 780578 905235